Willow Branch Road

Forbidden Love and Family Secrets

Tess Raynes

Pages By The Lake, LLC

Contents

Prologue: Unraveling the Past

Willow Branch Road was never more than a dirt path worn smooth by time and the heavy tread of secrets. The branches of the old oaks stretched over it like guardians, cloaking its quiet solitude in shadows, their whispered leaves speaking stories no one dared to voice aloud. The road itself, long forgotten by most, wound its way between two worlds: one filled with open skies, laughter, and the warmth of a family's love; the other, cloaked beneath the heavy silence of sacrifice, loyalty, and unspoken truths.

It was here, on the far edge of a small rural town, where two lives—separated by history, reputation, and the unyielding expectations of the world around them—found something rare. Something that was never meant to be.

In the 1930s, when the weight of the Great Depression hung heavy over the land, and every glance seemed laden with judgment, love was a thing one could not afford to take chances on. There was no room for fleeting romances, for desires that could tarnish names or scatter families to the wind. Yet, it was in the shadow of these very constraints that Evelyn Thompson and James Harris—two neighbors who lived just beyond the stretch of the long, winding road—found each other.

Theirs was not a love that could be celebrated openly. It was not a love born of dreams or declarations. No, theirs was the quiet kind. A kind that existed only in stolen glances across fields, in the corners of letters penned by trembling hands, in the soft murmurs of meetings hidden from the eyes of the world. Their love was bound by the walls of what could not be said, a love shrouded in quiet secrecy.

But love, even the kind that must be concealed, does not fade. It only burrows deeper into the heart, carving its place into the lives of those who carry it.

This is not just a story of love, though it is filled with it. This is a testament to the power of emotions that defy time, circumstance, and even life itself. It is the story of a forbidden romance—the quiet, unseen sacrifices that pass unnoticed by those too busy to look. It is the story of a family, of secrets passed down like heirlooms, carried from one generation to the next.

And it is the story of a granddaughter, years later, who stumbled across the whispers of those silences, pieced together what had been broken, and in doing so, found herself.

This is the legacy of Willow Branch Road—a legacy of love hidden, endured, and ultimately cherished across generations. Here, amid the tangled branches of the past, was a love that lived in silence and continued to live on long after the world had moved on.

And it is here, within these pages, where their story will finally be told.

Chapter One

The Discovery

E mma sat at the café, nursing her latte and half-listening to her friends, who were chattering excitedly about something.

"So, I sent in Max's DNA last week," Cara said, her eyes wide with excitement. "I can't wait to see if he's actually part wolf."

Emma raised an eyebrow and looked up from her phone. "Wait—DNA? For your dog?"

"Yeah! It's a thing now," Cara explained, laughing as she scrolled through her own phone. "You can send in a sample, and they tell you what breeds are in their lineage. It's all the rage."

"Seriously?" Emma leaned back in her chair, eyeing the group. "That's a thing now?"

"Oh, totally," chimed in Gina, who sat across from her with a mischievous grin. "I just got Luna's results back. Turns out she's mostly Labrador, but there's this random percentage of like... Dalmatian? Which makes zero sense, but it's kind of fun, you know?"

Emma's lips twitched into a smile as she shook her head. "You're all spending money to learn what your dogs are made of?"

"Hey, don't judge," Cara teased, pointing her finger at Emma. "You get to know their background! I mean, you learn stuff about their health, what they might be prone to, even weird quirks."

"Right, like why Max won't stop howling at the moon," Gina said with a snort. "You're about to find out he's one-quarter werewolf."

The table erupted in laughter, and Emma found herself smiling along, but her thoughts were elsewhere. As her friends swapped stories about their dogs' lineage—huskies with a trace of Siberian wolf, terriers with a dash of beagle—Emma found herself oddly fascinated.

She had always been curious about her family history. Growing up on the farm, her grandmother would tell stories about their ancestors coming over from England and the farmstead that had been passed down for generations. But the stories had always been a little vague, with gaps she never quite understood. Whenever she'd asked too many questions, her father would brush them aside, claiming the past wasn't as important as the future.

But what if there was more to the past? She never really thought about it beyond those stories, but maybe there were answers out there she hadn't even considered searching for.

"Hey, Emma," Cara said, breaking her from her thoughts. "You should do it, too! Not for a dog, obviously—but you know, one of those DNA tests. Ancestry, health stuff, the whole deal."

Emma blinked, caught off guard by the suggestion. "Me?"

"Yeah, why not?" Gina added, leaning in. "I mean, we're doing it for our dogs! It's kind of fun to know where you come from. Maybe you have some royal blood or something—Lady Emma of... wherever!"

They laughed again, but the idea had already planted itself in Emma's mind. She wasn't sure why she hadn't thought of it before. The past always seemed distant, foggy, like something that belonged in old photo albums. But now, hearing her friends talk about their dogs'

DNA tests with such enthusiasm, it struck her—if people could trace the lineage of their pets, surely she could do the same for herself.

"Yeah, maybe I will," Emma said slowly, her voice thoughtful.

Cara nudged her with a grin. "Do it! You never know what you'll find."

That was the thing, wasn't it? She didn't know what she might find. And that both intrigued and unsettled her.

After they finished lunch, Emma found herself driving home on autopilot, the thoughts of submitting a DNA test still swirling in her head. She imagined her grandmother's stories—the long stretches of farmland in Great Britain, the tough winters when they first came to America, the secrets her father never seemed to want to touch. Why had she never pushed more? And what if there was more to uncover than just a family tree? What about her health? What weird disease has been passed down to her?

Once inside her home, Emma kicked off her shoes and pulled out her laptop, her fingers hovering over the keyboard. She typed in "DNA test kits" and hit search. It wasn't long before she found a site offering ancestry results and health insights. She clicked through the testimonials, skimming over stories of people discovering long-lost relatives, unexpected heritage, new baby daddies, or medical information that had changed their lives.

There was a sense of anticipation as she added a kit to her cart. What if there was more to her story than the neat family narrative her grandmother had spun? What if the gaps in her father's evasions hinted at something deeper? What if she was related to someone famous in history? Or worse, Jack the Ripper? Her mind was running wild with possibilities.

She clicked "order" and leaned back, the decision made.

As the confirmation email popped up on her screen, Emma couldn't help but laugh at how this all started. Her friends were out there tracking down their dogs' genetic backgrounds, and here she was, about to do the same—but for herself.

It felt like a small step into the unknown, but for the first time, she felt a flicker of excitement. What had always seemed distant and unimportant now felt like a door waiting to be opened. Mystery lineages unfolded with just her spit in a tube.

Emma closed her laptop, smiling to herself. Maybe it was time to start asking the right questions.

***

Though the site claimed Emma would have her results within a week, she couldn't stop thinking about what little she knew about her past. The thoughts were almost obsessive, starting when she first woke up and popping into her head randomly throughout the day, no matter what else she might be doing.

Emma had always been fascinated by the things her grandmother, Evelyn, told her, even as a child. The evenings at her grandparents' farm stretched out, marked by the distant hum of crickets and the smell of fresh hay wafting through the open windows. Her grandmother would sit in her old armchair, her hands busy with knitting or smoothing out the edges of a quilt while her voice wove the past into something almost magical.

"Farming had been in the family for generations," Evelyn would say, her gaze softening as she recounted the hard times during the Depression when the land sustained them all. It was a source of pride, that farm.

But for all the tales of resilience, Emma noticed a strange gap in the stories—one she never quite understood as a child. The details surrounding her grandfather, Thomas, always felt faint, like an unfinished sentence. But her grandparents had been married forever, it seemed to Emma. She remembered celebrating their 50th anniversary when she was relatively young but would have to do the math to remember how long they'd been married when they died. With such a lasting marriage, shouldn't they know each other through and through?

It wasn't until Emma was much older—after both her parents and grandparents had passed—that the gnawing curiosity really set in. She had too many questions without answers and found it ironic that she hadn't thought to ask more about her family until it was too late.

Her brothers, of course, were no help. They'd always been restless during Evelyn's stories, more interested in doing anything else than sitting and listening. It had always been just Evelyn and Emma.

But Evelyn's stories had left gaps. All Emma had now were vague memories of her grandfather—the few stories that were told and retold mentioned him almost in passing. Like he was someone more functional than sentimental. Her father once told her he was a quiet man. *"Kept to himself mostly. Not much to say."* But there was something else, something unsaid, that Emma sensed every time the subject was broached.

The farm still stood, though the pasture was rented out to a neighbor for his cows and bailing the hay in the fields every year. She was unable to sell it, though, especially when she went to check on it and found its fields stretching out like memories frozen in time. Emma had inherited the house alongside her brothers. None of them cared much for it. They preferred to leave the past where it was—buried. But Emma had never been able to shake the feeling that there was something more beneath the surface of their family's story. She had always been the one to linger over old photos, to trace her fingers over the worn handwriting in Evelyn's recipe books, to wonder about the gaps in the family tree.

The DNA test had been an impulsive decision, sparked by nothing more than a vague curiosity about her ancestry and a bit of encouragement from her friends. Emma didn't expect much from it. After all, she knew where her family came from—both sides stretching back to settlers and farmers in Tennessee and Great Britain before that. The results would be nothing more than confirmation of what she already knew.

Or they might show something completely different. It wasn't unheard of for people to discover they had royalty or slavery in their heritage. The country was a melting pot, after all. Emma was almost excited about what she might discover... except for the nagging anxiety.

That split reaction is why she didn't tell her brothers she had done it. They wouldn't care, and honestly, Emma didn't think it would yield anything worth sharing. But what if the results came back with a different story to unfold? What if the information twisted her understanding of the past in ways she hadn't anticipated? Would she tell them then?

She'd have to, wouldn't she?

***

Emma's phone buzzed, a soft vibration against the wooden surface of her kitchen counter. She glanced at the screen while rinsing out her coffee mug, expecting another sale ad or a reminder about a doctor's appointment. But the subject line stopped her mid-motion:

Your DNA Results Are Ready

The mug slipped from her fingers, clattering into the sink with a sharp thud. She stood frozen for a moment, water rushing down the drain, her pulse quickening unexpectedly.

She reached for the phone, thumb hovering over the notification, but she didn't open it right away. Instead, she stared at the screen, her reflection blurred on the glossy surface.

Why did her heart feel like it had just skipped a beat?

It's just a DNA test, she reminded herself. A fun thing. Her friends teased her about joining the trend and convinced her it would be interesting to see her ancestry in percentages and maybe uncover some quirky bits of family history. Something like being 2% Viking or learning her great-great-grandmother had been an Irish rebel.

So why did she feel like this?

Emma pressed her lips together, locking her phone without reading the email. She stepped back, drying her hands on a towel, trying to shake the sudden unease creeping up her spine.

She wasn't sure what she expected, but whatever it was, it felt bigger than some pie chart of her family heritage. She couldn't pinpoint why, but the thought of opening those results felt like cracking open a door she wasn't ready to walk through yet.

For as long as she could remember, her family had been close-knit. The Harris family was strong, grounded in years of shared history, stories passed down over cozy nights around the fireplace, and holiday gatherings where her grandparents sat at the head of the table. Emma grew up knowing exactly who she was.

Her grandparents on both sides had been constants in her life, towering figures of warmth and tradition. Evelyn, her grandmother, had taught her how to knead dough and tend to the small herb garden in the back of the farm. And her grandfather, Thomas, would sit on the porch in the evenings, telling her about the old days when the farm was his everything, how he'd spend all his time out there, from sun up to sun down, working the land. Their stories were stitched together with familiar threads of loyalty, hard work, and devotion to the family's land.

They'd been there for every birthday, every holiday, every graduation. She had pictures with each of them—happy, smiling, whole. She could still remember the smell of her grandfather's old leather chair, the one he sat in while smoking his pipe, and the sound of her grandmother's laugh echoing through the kitchen.

So why did the sight of that unopened email feel like a weight in her chest? What was this prickling sense that there might be something in the results she wasn't prepared for?

She picked up the phone again, unlocking it with a swipe. The email stared back at her. Emma's thumb hovered over the message, her mind racing. It didn't make sense. She wasn't uncovering some deep, mysterious past. She knew her lineage—knew where her grandparents came from, where the farm had originated. The farm had been in the family for generations, her father used to say, almost with a sense of pride.

But that was it, wasn't it? The farm was a monument to their legacy. A stable, unchanging place where the past wasn't just remembered; it was lived. And maybe that's what unnerved her. The idea that something in these results could shift that steady foundation. A crack in the narrative she'd grown up with.

She shook her head, feeling ridiculous. "It's just a test," she muttered aloud, trying to convince herself. A glance at the clock told her she was running late for her afternoon book club meeting with friends.

Emma sighed, locking the phone and placing it face down on the counter again. She'd open the email later, she decided, as if delaying it would make the odd sensation in her gut disappear.

As she hurried to get ready, a nagging thought stayed with her—quiet, but persistent.

Why did it feel like she was about to find out something that wasn't supposed to be known?

She didn't have any logical reason to feel that way. She'd known her grandparents and her parents, known them well. There was no reason to think any secrets were buried in the past, no family mysteries lingering in the shadows. No long lost sister she never knew about, although it would be nice to have a sister. Her father, her uncles—they were solid men, hardworking and straightforward, just like her grandparents had been.

And yet, there it was—this whisper of doubt, the unsettling feeling that maybe there was more to the story than she'd ever been told.

Later that night, as Emma sat alone on the couch, the email still unread, she picked up her phone again. The screen glowed in the dark room, the subject line as bright as ever:

Your DNA Results Are Ready

Her hand trembled slightly as she hovered over it again.

Then she clicked.

***

Emma's eyes scanned the page, first looking for the percentage breakdown, wondering if she'd find a surprising heritage. Then, the names appeared—relatives she recognized, a cousin here, a distant aunt there. But there, near the top, was a name she hadn't expected.

James Thompson.

Her heart stuttered, and her fingers hovered over the trackpad as she clicked on his profile. Mr. Thompson? The neighbor? She shook her head, trying to clear the confusion. It didn't make sense. She'd known him since childhood and visited his farm with her brothers when they were kids.

She clicked through the connection details, her breath shallow, her chest tightening. The results were clear—biological grandfather. The words hung there, stark and undeniable. She leaned back in her chair, her eyes widening as her mind raced to keep up with what she was reading.

"How...?" she whispered, though no one was there to answer her.

Emma stared at the screen in disbelief; her eyes focused only on the name that appeared in bold: James Thompson. Mr. Thompson had lived down the road from her grandmother's farm for as long as Emma had been alive. His place was tucked behind a row of poplar trees on Willow Branch Road. He had been a fixture in her childhood, a quiet neighbor who always waved when she passed by on her bike, his face a permanent fixture of her summer memories.

But grandfather? Emma's breath caught in her throat. She clicked through the results again, hoping there had been some mistake, some glitch in the system. But there it was—undeniable. James Thompson, the man who lived next door, the man whose farm had bordered her grandmother's all those years, was her biological grandfather.

The world shifted under her feet, the weight of the revelation sinking into her chest like a stone.

How could this be?

Her hand instinctively went to her mouth as she thought of her father. Could he have known? Had anyone known? Memories of her childhood flashed in rapid succession—summer afternoons spent on her grandmother's porch, the smell of fresh bread and hay mingling in the air, the soft hum of cicadas in the distance. Mr. Thompson had been a fixture, always nearby but never particularly present. He was just part of the backdrop of her youth.

But now... he was her grandfather.

Emma stood abruptly, the chair scraping across the worn kitchen floor. She paced to the window, staring out at the familiar landscape of her back garden, but her imagination was picturing a place miles away. She could almost see the fields stretched out under the gray sky, peaceful and unchanged. She had always loved that view, the sense of permanence the farm offered, a place where everything stayed the same, generation after generation. Now, it felt like the earth had shifted beneath her feet.

The revelation hit her like a cold wind. Mr. Thompson wasn't just the neighbor; he was part of her, a piece of her family she had never known existed. And if he was her grandfather, then her grandmother—Evelyn—had been involved in something much more complicated than the simple life she had always portrayed.

Emma's breath caught as she thought of Evelyn, her quiet, kind grandmother who had always treated her with such care when she visited. Had she lived with this secret her whole life? The weight of it must have been suffocating. Did her dad know? Surely, he'd known.

She turned back to the laptop, the screen still glowing with the revelation. Her mind raced to piece together the fragments—her father, her uncle, her grandparents, the life they had all built around a secret buried deep in the soil of that land.

The farm had always been a place of stability, a place where roots ran deep, and history was etched into every beam of the house. But now it would be different. Emma knew she needed to go there as she continued unearthing this secret. She needed to be somewhere she knew better than anywhere else in the world while she tried to determine how much of the past she truly understood.

Mr. Thompson... her biological grandfather. The man who had lived just down the road all her life, who had waved at her across fences, watched her grow up from the sidelines. He had known. He must have known.

The realization sat heavy in her chest, like a stone. She sank back into her chair, staring blankly at the screen. The name didn't disappear, no matter how much she wished it would. James Thompson. The truth was there, and it had changed everything.

She tried to remember conversations she had with Mr. Thompson, the neighbor—trying to think if there were any signs she did not pick up on. Or maybe he didn't know either, and only her grandmother did. Since DNA testing wasn't available back then, maybe she didn't know who Emma's dad's father was. So many unanswered questions, and now did she even want to know the answers? Did she want to taint her memories?

Emma closed her eyes, trying to make sense of it all. There had to be more to the story. There always was. But how much had been hidden? How much had been left unsaid, locked away in hearts too burdened to speak?

As the weight of the revelation settled into her bones, Emma knew one thing for certain—nothing about her family was as it seemed.

Chapter Two

The Hidden Letters

The late afternoon sun filtered through the large bay window, casting long shadows across the kitchen floor. Emma sat at her table, the DNA test results printed in front of her, untouched for what felt like hours. Her fingers traced the edges of the paper as if, somehow, she could find the answers she sought in the texture of the page.

The sound of a gentle knock startled her. Then, she heard the front door creaking open. Her brother Rob walked in, his boots heavy on the worn hardwood. He glanced at her, his expression unreadable, and gave a brief nod before grabbing a glass from her cabinet.

"Rob," she said, her voice softer than she intended. "We need to talk."

He poured water from the tap, took a long sip, and turned to face her, leaning against the counter. "About what?" he asked, his tone clipped.

Emma took a breath, trying to steady herself. "About the DNA test. About what I found out."

Rob's face didn't change. He simply put the glass down and folded his arms across his chest. "Let me tell you what I think about that," he said, his voice as hard as his posture. "Nothing. It doesn't matter. There's nothing to talk about."

"How can you say that?" Emma's frustration bubbled to the surface. "I'm trying to understand where we come from, where I come from."

"We come from the farm, Emma. From Mom and Dad. That's all there is." He turned toward the door as if the conversation had ended, but Emma wasn't ready to let him walk away.

"Rob, wait," she called after him. He paused but didn't turn back. "Dave and Mike are on their way. Let's all talk about this. Please?"

He stood there, silent, his back to her, the tension in his shoulders visible even from across the room.

"Did you know?" Her voice broke, and she hated the vulnerability that slipped through. "Why was it kept a secret?"

Rob sighed, the sound heavy in the stillness of the kitchen. "I didn't know. I suspected. I heard some talk. But Emma... Some things are better left in the past."

Before Emma could respond, the back door opened, and Dave walked in, smiling, clueless about the point of this rare sibling meeting. "What's going on?" he asked, his smile fading as he looked between them. Rob caught his eye and shot him a look; then Dave nodded in understanding.

Emma threw her arms up in exasperation. "You too? Thanks a lot, guys. Really close family bonds we have here."

"You're always asking questions you don't want to know the answers to," Rob muttered.

"Let's be honest, I already got my answers," Emma shot back, her voice sharp now. She turned to Dave, hoping for some understanding.

"I just want to find out why. Why did it happen? Why was it a secret? Why couldn't we just have been told when Mom and Dad were here to tell us about it? Why did I have to find out this way?"

Just then, Mike walked in, the latecomer as he typically was. His expression was more detached and calm than his other brothers', as if he had just come in to see what the fuss was about but didn't want to get involved. "What's all this?" he asked, looking between his siblings.

Dave rolled his eyes at his younger brother and rubbed the back of his neck, avoiding Emma's gaze. "It's not that simple, Emma."

"Not that simple?" She stood up, the chair scraping against the floor. "I found out from a piece of paper, Dave. Not from you, not from Rob. A piece of paper."

Mike glanced at the results spread on the table, confusion etched on his face. "What paper?" he asked, genuinely curious but not fully engaged in the tense atmosphere.

"Just something I discovered about... us," Emma replied, her voice trembling. She turned back to Dave. "I just want to know the truth about my own family."

Rob turned then, his eyes hard. "What good would it do, Emma? Stirring all this up, dragging our family's name through the mud? It won't change anything."

"It changes everything for me," Emma said, her voice trembling with the weight of it all. "I can't just forget what I know now."

Mike shifted uncomfortably, sensing the rising tension. "I mean, can't we just let it go? If it's in the past..." he began, but Emma cut him off.

"No! This is my life!" she cried. "You all keep acting like it's some old story that doesn't matter. It matters to me."

Dave put a hand on her shoulder, but she shrugged it off, too raw for comfort. "We get it, Emma," he said. "But some secrets... they were meant to protect us."

Emma's chest tightened. "To protect you, maybe. But I'm not a child anymore. I don't need protecting from the truth."

Rob's jaw tightened, and for a moment, Emma thought he might say something more, but instead, he just shook his head. "Let it go, Emma," he said quietly. "Let the past stay where it belongs. It's what Dad wanted, and it was his story to tell."

He walked out of the kitchen without another word, his boots echoing through the empty hallway. Dave hesitated, standing in the silence between them.

"Dave," Emma whispered, her voice barely holding steady. "Please, help me understand."

But Dave only gave her a sad smile, the kind that said he wished things were different but knew they never would be. "Sometimes, Emma... you just have to accept things the way they are."

He left, too, the door closing softly behind him. Emma stood alone in the kitchen, the sunlight fading as the shadows grew longer. The silence felt heavier now, more suffocating, as if the walls themselves held the weight of the secrets her family had kept buried for so long.

Mike lingered in the doorway, unsure of what to do. "Emma," he finally said, his voice softer. "I don't know what's going on, but I'm here if you want to talk."

She looked at him, appreciating the offer but feeling overwhelmed. "Thanks, Mike," she replied quietly. "I just... I need to figure this out."

He nodded, giving her the space she needed before stepping back into the hallway, leaving her alone with her thoughts. Emma looked down at the paper in front of her, the truth written there in black and white, undeniable. But the answers she wanted, the closure she needed, would have to come from somewhere else.

Rob was wrong; she knew it. This wasn't her father's story. It might have influenced how he grew up, but this story belonged to her grandmother and Mr. Thompson. And Emma needed to piece this together so she could read the complete book.

***

The laptop warmed Emma's thighs as she stared at the screen, her fingers hovering over the keyboard. The smell of freshly brewed coffee lingered in the air, but she had forgotten about the mug that sat untouched on the table beside the couch. On the computer, the search box blinked expectantly, its blankness matching the knot of uncertainty in her chest.

After the interaction with her brothers, she wondered if it truly was best to leave things alone. After all, her grandparents were dead. Her parents were dead. Did it matter who her grandfather really was?

It did matter to her. After all, she already knew who he was. Now, she wanted to know more about the why and the how. But she had promised herself she wouldn't dig too deep.

And yet here she was, staring at census records and faded, grainy images of gravestones, tracing the invisible threads that connected the Harris and Thompson families. Each click of the trackpad felt heavier than the last, like stepping into quicksand she couldn't pull herself out of. The DNA test results cracked the door open, but it was Emma who pushed it wide, desperate to understand what lay on the other side.

The Thompson family tree was a gnarled and complex web, much like her own. She had known the Thompsons her whole life—or she thought she had. They'd always been next door, in the background of big town gatherings each summer at the farm. But now, every name and every branch on the genealogy chart felt charged with secrets and meaning. She scrolled through birth certificates and property records, her eyes catching on a familiar date.

Her grandmother had always described that year like a natural disaster. The Great Depression had its claws deep in the country, and while many families had fallen into despair, her grandparents' farm had somehow survived. They had weathered the storm—kept everything running even as their neighbors faltered.

Emma clicked on a census record, her breath catching as she saw the familiar names. Evelyn Harris. Thomas Harris. And there, just a few lines down, was James Thompson. He had lived just down the road, not far enough for the space between them to matter.

A flicker of something itched at the back of her mind. What had drawn James and her grandmother together? What had bound them so tightly, enough that they would keep it secret for an entire lifetime?

She leaned back in her chair, rubbing her temples as her mind churned over the possibilities. It wasn't just an affair; the connection ran beyond that. The land. The shared history. They had lived side by side, their families intertwined long before anyone had known or cared about DNA.

Emma scrolled further, her eyes narrowing at the mention of a land deed. The Thompson farm had been in the family since the late 1800s, just like her grandmother's, passed down through generations. She clicked on the document, watching as the details unfurled—acres sold, cattle exchanged, signatures penned by long-dead relatives.

Her gaze lingered on the signature: James Thompson. The same hand that wrote that was the same hand that had held her grandmother's in secret.

Suddenly, a memory flashed before her eyes—her grandmother's laughter, warm and musical, as she served pie to Mr. Thompson during one of the many summer picnics they had all shared. Emma had been a child then, oblivious to the undercurrents, the glances that passed between them. She had simply seen two neighbors, two families enjoying the warmth of a southern evening. Her grandmother had always been a caregiver, a natural hostess, making all her guests feel at home.

But now, she knew better.

Her fingers moved to the keyboard, searching for more. She followed the thread further, discovering that the Thompson farm had almost been lost during the Depression. But in 1934, a mysterious loan had kept it afloat. A loan that had no official source.

She leaned closer, her pulse quickening. Was it her grandmother? Had Evelyn helped them in some way, using her family's meager safety net to save the Thompsons? It wouldn't have been unusual. Helping neighbors during that time didn't mean you were having an affair; it was simply how communities came together during hardship. But it wasn't just a kindness, was it? No—this was a lifeline thrown across the road, a bridge between two hearts that had always been connected.

Emma sat back, staring at the screen, her heart skipping beats in her chest. She had uncovered some ties, yes, but she still didn't have the full picture. This felt like she was just tugging at one end of the string. She didn't see her grandmother as an adulterer, sleeping around town. There had to be more to the story. She just knew it. She needed there to be more to the story. Knowing her grandmother and the Thompsons had been linked for years was just the foundation of their history.

How much had Evelyn sacrificed? Money, yes, but what about her love, her life, her freedom to be with the man she loved? Had she loved him? Had he loved her? And why had that love been so deeply buried, concealed under layers of propriety and silence?

Emma knew she had to explore further. There was more here than just a tangled family tree. There was a story—a love story that had shaped generations, even if no one had dared to speak of it.

The truth was out there, buried in old paper and whispered family history, and she was determined to unearth every last fragment. She knew that internet research would only take her so far. She needed to go back to the place where it happened. Not only could she look through the things her grandmother saved, but she could also access town records if they'd survived the passage of time.

There was only one way to find out. Emma was going back to Willow Branch Road.

***

Emma pulled her car off the main road, her tires crunching over the gravel as she turned onto Willow Branch Road. The narrow, winding lane, now overgrown with wild blackberry bushes and leaning oak trees, felt more like a forgotten path than the road she'd traveled countless times as a child. Back then, it had seemed so ordinary, just the last boring, dusty stretch leading to her grandmother's farm, and the excitement she knew awaited her on the family's farm. Now, the journey itself hummed with excitement. Emma felt like this road was a secret artery, connecting her not only to the farm but to something more profound.

As she drove slowly down the unpaved road, her eyes traced the familiar landscape: the rolling hills, the patches of corn that still stretched along the fence line. The scent of honeysuckle drifted through the open window, taking her back to long, sticky summers spent chasing fireflies and weaving flower crowns with her brothers.

But this time, the air felt heavier, as if the road itself held its breath, waiting for her to remember something she hadn't yet fully understood. She knew there was something hiding beneath those blissful, innocent memories, and it was almost enough to make her stop and turn the car around. Maybe her brothers were right; maybe she should leave well enough alone. How many people had wholesome, beautiful memories like this?

However, she knew those memories were already tainted. She'd never be able to find peace in them again, so she might as well find the truth. There was always the possibility that it was much better than she was expecting.

Emma stopped at the bend in the road where the trees opened up just enough to reveal the Thompson farm. She had played there a time or two as a child, running through their barn with her brothers, her laughter mingling with theirs. It had almost felt like home as much as her grandmother's place, but she had never questioned why. She thought it was because she was a kid, adored by everyone older, given free rein of the properties so they could enjoy spending time outside and give the adults time to talk without interruptions. She'd never wondered why her father grew quiet when they passed by the Thompsons' place when they reached this stretch. She never thought too hard about why Mr. Thompson would look at her and her brothers with those steady, unreadable eyes.

She parked her car near the wooden fence, its slats weathered and splintered by years of wind and sun. Stepping out, she took in the familiar sight of her grandparents' farmhouse, its white paint now peeling and the windows slightly dull. The place had aged, much like the memories she carried with her, but it still stood solid, a monument to her family's resilience.

Her feet carried her toward the front porch, and as she stepped onto the creaking boards, she couldn't help but glance toward the path leading to the barn. How many times had she skipped down that same trail, hand in hand with her grandmother?

Evelyn's voice echoed in her mind—soft, with that hint of British accent she never fully lost. "Stay close now, Emma. The world's bigger than it seems when you're small."

She hadn't known then how true those words were. The world of her childhood had been simple, safe, and she was grateful for it. But now everything seemed tainted, and she wasn't sure how to feel about her past. After all, she never had a chance to know the truth; she'd had to discover it on her own. It wasn't until the DNA test results arrived that everything began to unravel. Mr. Thompson, not Thomas, had been her grandfather. The man who raised her father wasn't the man who fathered him. Her last name was not her biological last name. She had Thomas's last name. Weird, what did that mean for her, now? The secrets Evelyn had carried weren't the quiet, private ones Emma had once assumed, but the heavy, tangled truths that spanned generations.

Her fingers brushed the rough wood of the porch railing, and she turned her gaze back to Willow Branch Road. The line between the two farms was clearer to her now. That road hadn't just connected two families; it had divided them. And yet, in some way, it had also woven their lives together. The same road she'd wandered as a child had carried Evelyn back and forth, bridging the gap between the life she had and the one she couldn't claim.

Emma closed her eyes, trying to picture it—her grandmother walking this same road in the early morning, her heart heavy with the weight of choices she could never fully share. Did she glance at the Thompson farm the way Emma had today? Did she feel that same tug of longing, of love, of guilt?

A sudden gust of wind sent a scattering of leaves across the dirt road, and Emma shivered, wrapping her arms around herself. The weight of the secret pressed on her, just as it must have weighed on Evelyn. And yet, it wasn't anger or betrayal that Emma felt—it was a strange sense of understanding. The choices Evelyn had made, the sacrifices, had shaped their family in ways Emma was only now beginning to grasp.

She turned to head inside, pausing in the hallway connecting the front rooms to the kitchen and dining area. She glanced upward at the ceiling, her eyes catching the small, square wooden door to the attic.

With a soft grunt, Emma pulled down the attic stairs, the ladder creaking as it unfolded in front of her. The smell of dust and old wood greeted her as she climbed, each step echoing in the narrow hallway below. She reached the attic, a space that had always seemed mysterious in her childhood, filled with trunks and boxes that hinted at long-buried secrets. The slanted ceiling made the room feel smaller, the wooden beams exposed and splintered with age. Cobwebs clung to the rafters, and the faint light from a single round window cast ghostly shadows across the cluttered space.

Emma's breath caught in her throat as she stepped further in, her eyes scanning the familiar jumble of forgotten objects—old furniture draped in dusty sheets, crates filled with yellowed papers, and a large, timeworn cedar chest pushed against the back wall.

She knelt down beside it, her fingers trailing over the rough surface of the wood. The brass hinges had turned green with age, and as she lifted the heavy lid, the smell of cedar mixed with something older—memories, perhaps, or the weight of the past pressing down on her. Inside, neatly folded under her grandmother's wedding gown and an array of handmade quilts, was the small box she had never uncovered before. It was worn, like everything else, its edges softened by time.

Emma's fingers trembled as she carefully opened the aged box, revealing a stack of letters, brittle with time and bound with a delicate piece of twine. The paper, yellowed and fragile, seemed to sigh as she lifted the top letter, unfolding it with reverence. Her grandmother's graceful, looping handwriting stretched across the page, each word written with the unmistakable tenderness of a woman in love. But it was the name at the top of each letter that made Emma catch her breath: James.

James Thompson.

A chill ran through her as she scanned the lines, words whispering of a hidden love—something unthinkable. Had she not been holding the proof in her hands? These letters revealed a side of her grandmother Emma had never imagined: not merely a woman of scandalous reputation, but a woman with a heart entwined in a love so deep it had endured in secret for decades. Emma felt a weight settle in her chest as though these unspoken truths were pressing against her, demanding to be acknowledged.

In the stillness of the attic, the house seemed to hold its breath. The creak of the floorboards below mingled with the wind whistling softly through the cracks. She could almost hear her grandmother's voice—a soft, familiar murmur wrapped in memory and longing.

Seated on the dusty attic floor, Emma clutched the letters like precious relics, each one a piece of a long-buried story. Her grandmother's life, her choices, her love—they were all woven into these delicate pages, tied to Mr. Thompson, the man from the farm down the road. And now, Emma realized, her own life was bound to theirs as well. These letters were more than a hidden love story; they were a legacy, an inheritance of resilience, passion, and secrets she was only just beginning to understand.

The house creaked below her, the sounds of settling wood and distant memories weaving together as Emma sat on the attic floor, holding the past in her hands. Each letter was another piece of the puzzle, but it was a puzzle that felt impossible to complete without someone else's truth. Her grandmother's life, her choices—they were all tied to Mr. Thompson, to the farm down the road, and now, to Emma herself.

For a long moment, Emma simply sat there, staring at the letters. The farmhouse, quiet and filled with the echoes of a family long gone, seemed to hold its breath, waiting for her to decide what to do next.

When she finally faced the truth, Emma knew the answers wouldn't come from Rob's stubborn silence, Dave's half-hearted attempts to smooth things over, or Mike's indifference. No, the real story had always lived here, in these letters and in whatever was left of her grandmother's voice, waiting for someone willing to uncover it.

Emma looked at the stack in her hands, so many letters, each one a testament to a love hidden in plain sight. How long had this gone on? she wondered, feeling the years stretch out with each fragile page she touched. As she read, she felt her grandmother's pain pour through every word—a love both cherished and forbidden, cloaked in secrecy and longing.

A tear slipped down Emma's cheek. Her grandmother's anguish felt so vivid, so present, that she wanted nothing more than to be in her arms again, to tell her it was all right, that she was understood. But here, in these letters, her grandmother was speaking across time, sharing the life she'd kept hidden, and Emma knew it was up to her to honor it. With every letter, she drew closer, piecing together the love and sacrifice that had shaped her grandmother's life—and now, her own.

Chapter Three

Dear Evelyn

March 10, 1933

Dear Evelyn,

I find myself sitting here this evening, a pencil in hand, struggling to express the thoughts that have taken root in my heart. The wind is blowing fiercely outside, and I can hear it whipping around the edges of the house. It's strange how the wind can carry so many memories with it, stirring up dust and time in the most unexpected ways.

I've thought often of that first day we met. I remember the smell of the air that morning—the sweet, damp scent of late spring—and how it lingered with me long after. I recall walking along the edge of my property, surveying the fields, when I saw you standing at the edge of your porch. There was something about the way the sunlight caught in your hair, the way you stood so quietly as if you had always belonged to the land, just as the trees and the river did.

At the time, I thought I was merely looking at a neighbor—a woman I had never met but who, somehow, seemed more familiar than any stranger ought to. I couldn't have known then how much my life was about to change, how it would shift in the most beautiful and painful way.

You bringing bread was the welcoming I didn't know I needed, but it made me think that maybe I could make it on this land after all. In the months that followed, there were times when our paths crossed, small moments in town, a chance meeting at the market, or catching each other's eyes at church.

I remember the way you always smiled when I approached, as though you had been waiting for my company, though you never said a word about it. There was a quiet understanding between us, something that felt more profound than anything I had ever experienced. I would see you out by the garden, tending to flowers or picking vegetables, and every glance we exchanged seemed to hold a conversation all its own.

I can't help but think back to that first meeting, Evelyn. How strange it was, how easy it was to be near you. I could talk to you without effort—no hesitations, no careful words—like you were someone I had always known, even though we were strangers. And when you spoke, you made me feel as if I was the only person in the world who mattered.

There is so much I wish I could tell you, but even now, after everything, I find myself hesitating. Perhaps it is the weight of what we share, what we are becoming, that makes me unsure of the right words. But I must tell you this: I've never felt this way about anyone, not in all my life. I never expected it—never thought that someone could make me feel so... whole. And yet here you are, pulling me into your world as though it were always meant to be.

I think of you more than I ever thought possible, of your laugh, your kindness, your steady presence. I find myself wishing for more moments with you, wishing that the time between us wasn't so long, that we didn't have to hide behind a mask of polite words when I long to speak to you of things that no one else can understand.

You are the first thought in my day and the last at night. I want you to know that you have changed me, Evelyn. In ways I can't explain, but in ways I can feel every day, in every beat of my heart.

I know the world is a harsh one, and there is much we must both face in the days ahead. But for now, I will treasure these quiet moments between us. I will hold onto the knowledge that I have you in my life, even if only in small pieces.

Yours always,

James

Chapter Four

The Meeting

E velyn brushed a few strands of hair away from her face and set the last plate on the table, taking a step back to admire her work. It probably wouldn't seem like much by city standards, but for a small family with only what the land offered, it was a feast. She'd managed to pull together a pot roast with thick cuts of potatoes and carrots, buttered green beans, and biscuits, still steaming from the stove.

"Smells real nice, Ma," Seth said as he climbed into his chair. His sandy hair was sticking up in all directions, still wild from his afternoon playing by the creek.

She reached over and smoothed his hair with a soft laugh. "Thank you, sweetheart. Glad you're hungry."

Thomas settled into his chair across from Seth, nodding absently. His mind was already somewhere out on the land. She could see it in the way he reached for his fork without a glance at the food, already chewing before she had a chance to sit down.

They ate in silence, save for the clinking of forks on their plates. Evelyn tried to savor the food, but her appetite dimmed watching them eat with a hurried efficiency, as if they were fulfilling a chore rather than sharing a meal. She looked to Seth, his cheeks flushed with excitement as he watched his father.

"Pa?" Seth asked between bites. "You think maybe I could come along after supper? You know, help with the tilling?"

Thomas wiped his mouth and nodded. "We could use another set of hands, I reckon. That back field's still got a ways to go if we want it ready by planting season."

Seth's grin was instant, lighting up his face as he shoveled the rest of his food. Evelyn felt a pinch in her chest, part pride and part sadness. He was eager to be like his father, to follow him into the fields as though the soil held answers Evelyn couldn't provide.

"You sure you don't want to stay a while longer?" Evelyn asked, keeping her voice soft. "No hurry tonight, is there?"

Thomas looked up as if noticing her for the first time that evening. He hesitated, eyes flicking to Seth's eager expression, then shook his head. "Sorry, Evie. Work won't wait."

The childish nickname made her bristle, but she kept her mouth closed. She'd known Thomas for so long, but despite growing older together and starting a family, she felt like he still thought of her as a little girl.

Their own little boy pushed back from the table, barely able to sit still as Thomas drained his water glass and rose.

Evelyn watched them both stand, her hands folded in her lap. She forced a smile as they left the kitchen, footsteps fading through the hallway and out the door. For a few moments, she stayed in the silence they left behind, the ticking of the clock on the wall the only company.

The food on her plate had long gone cold, and though she managed a few bites, her appetite seemed to vanish altogether. She wrapped the remains in cloth, setting them aside for tomorrow, then cleared the table.

She started scrubbing at a pot with a rag, watching the last of the evening light disappear over the fields. Surely Thomas and Seth would come back in soon since it was getting too dark to till.

Her hands stilled as something caught her eye: not the figures of her husband and son, but lights. She peered out of the window until she realized they were the headlights of an old pickup rolling slowly along the road before coming to a stop in front of the farmhouse next door. She squinted, leaning closer to the glass, but the truck was too far to make out details, only that it looked old and travel-worn, its headlights casting long beams over the dusty drive.

Footsteps sounded in the hall, and she turned as Thomas entered the kitchen, dusted in soil from the field and already moving toward the stairs, unbuckling his suspenders. She dried her hands on her apron and called out.

"Thomas," she began, her voice soft, almost tentative. "Did you see the truck out by the place next door? Looked like someone was moving in."

He shrugged, running a hand through his graying hair. "Oh, yes. Think someone's moving in. Not sure who yet."

Evelyn felt her curiosity flare up, but Thomas was already at the door, his hand on the worn frame. She opened her mouth, but he turned, already nodding goodnight.

"Don't you think we should go over, meet 'em properly?" she asked, her words rushing out before he could leave. "Maybe tomorrow. I could bake something, take it over."

Thomas just gave a quick nod, half his attention already elsewhere. "If you like. I'll be up early, though—don't go waiting on me." And with that, he turned, his heavy footsteps echoing up the wooden stairs.

Evelyn watched him go, her enthusiasm tempered but not extinguished. She glanced back at the empty yard outside. The headlights of the truck were gone, leaving only the soft glow of a lamp shining from the farmhouse window. A new family, she thought, trying to picture who they might be—farmers like them or maybe city folk who didn't yet know what they'd signed up for.

Determined now, Evelyn returned to the counter and rummaged through her pantry, setting out the few remaining ingredients she had. Some flour, the last handful of walnuts she'd been saving, a bit of sugar, and dates she'd stowed away for a special occasion. A small smile crept across her lips. It wasn't much, but it would make a fine date nut bread if she could stretch it just right.

As she worked, her hands kneading the dough and folding in the chopped dates and nuts; she felt a warmth in her chest she hadn't known in a long while—a reminder of the first time she'd baked for Thomas, bringing him a slice of pie as an excuse just to see him. She wrapped the dough carefully, setting it aside to rise, and let her gaze drift back to the window. Tomorrow, she'd bring a loaf over to the new neighbors, a gesture of welcome and maybe... maybe a small spark of something new in her life that had started feeling so stale.

When she finally climbed the stairs in the dark of night, Thomas was already asleep, his soft snores filling the room he shared with Seth. Evelyn moved quietly to her room, taking a moment to appreciate having everything arranged just as she wanted. She especially loved the delicate doilies on the dresser under the kerosene lamp she lit to have a bit of light as she prepared for bed. She couldn't help but think of the farmhouse next door and the folks who might soon fill it with voices, laughter, and warmth. With a final glance out the bedroom window, she closed her eyes, picturing their faces, wondering what might come of a simple loaf of bread and a neighbor's visit.

***

The bread was still warm from its morning bake when Evelyn wrapped it tightly in a linen towel. She slipped it into her basket and set out across the field. The air was crisp, carrying the faint scent of freshly turned earth, and in the distance, she could see Thomas bent over, his back to her as he worked in the rows of beans. She walked briskly, feeling a slight thrill as she neared the edge of their property and Willow Branch Road, the narrow dirt path that twisted its way over to the farmhouse next door.

The house stood quiet and still, framed by towering oaks, its brick red paint weathered and peeling. She glanced back over her shoulder, half-expecting to see Thomas looking after her, but he was entirely absorbed in his work. Seth was at school, and her morning chores were done. She took a steadying breath, straightened her posture, and rapped her knuckles on the door.

It took a moment, and she was about to knock again, but then the door opened. A tall figure stood in the doorway—a man. His hair was dark, combed neatly back, and his eyes, strikingly blue, regarded her with a quiet curiosity. Evelyn's words caught in her throat, and she quickly cleared it, feeling a sudden warmth rise to her cheeks. She hadn't expected him.

"Oh! Good morning," she managed, a polite smile pulling at her lips. "I, uh... I just wanted to welcome y'all to the neighborhood." She held up the basket with the bread. "Brought something fresh from the oven."

The man's gaze dropped to the basket, and he smiled—a gentle, grateful sort of smile that softened the sharp angles of his face. "Thank you, ma'am," he said, his voice warm and rich, though she caught a hint of surprise in it. "I appreciate it. We've just barely got settled in." He stepped back, motioning her inside. "Would you like to come in?"

"Oh, I wouldn't want to intrude," she replied quickly, though the offer lingered temptingly. She'd meant only to hand off the bread and exchange a few pleasantries, but this stranger's openness made her curious.

"Not an intrusion at all," he insisted. "Haven't had much company out here yet. I'm James Thompson. Come on in."

Evelyn lingered at the door, but Mr. Thompson turned and went down the hall, so she followed him.

"You're from the farm over yonder, right?" he asked once they reached the kitchen, his hands motioning toward the land beyond the road that separated their two properties.

"Yes, that's right," Evelyn replied, her hands instinctively smoothing the skirt of her dress. "I've lived there all of my life." She glanced at him then, realizing she hadn't properly introduced herself. "I'm Evelyn Harris," she added, feeling a little silly for not starting with the basics.

"The weather's been good to us lately," he said in a friendly tone. "Been working the fields all day. You?"

Evelyn nodded, her fingers fiddling with the edge of her sleeve. "Oh, you know. Same old. Gardens to tend, chickens to feed. It never ends."

Mr. Thompson smiled, and the warmth in his expression made Evelyn feel a little lighter. "I reckon it doesn't. Doesn't sound like a lot of rest in your day."

"No, there's never much of that, Mr. Thompson," she replied.

"Call me James," he said. "What would you do with your downtime?"

Evelyn hesitated for just a second. She wasn't used to talking casually like this, especially to a man who wasn't her husband. But something in James's voice made her feel as though he might actually listen, unlike Thomas, who rarely seemed to notice anything that wasn't right in front of him.

"Well," she said slowly, "I've been thinking about how I'd like to write stories. I write letters to my sister, who moved across the country. And I think I make farm life sound pretty interesting. I bet I could spin a story. But that sounds silly."

"Writing?" James said quickly, his eyes meeting hers with an intensity that made her pulse quicken. "That doesn't sound silly at all. That's important."

Evelyn blinked. She hadn't expected him to understand—most people she talked to brushed her whims aside.

"So," James said, breaking the silence, "tell me about yourself, Evelyn. What's it like, living on a farm like that? I've just now moved from the city to have this land over here. I've always wondered what it'd be like to run the same kind of place you do."

Evelyn was caught off guard by his question. Most men, especially the ones in town, never asked her about her life. They assumed they already knew or didn't care enough to inquire.

She hesitated, then smiled, surprised at how easily the words came. "Well, there's a lot of work, as I said. But there's something about the rhythm of it. The seasons change, and you change with them. There's a peace in the work, even if it's hard. And the land, it's been there so long. It's... it's like part of who I am."

"That's a beautiful way of putting it," James said, his voice soft, his eyes intent on her face.

Evelyn felt her heart skip a beat. She wasn't used to this—being treated like her words mattered... like she mattered.

Time passed quickly, and she realized she needed to get home to have lunch ready when Seth came back from school. She'd have to call Thomas in from the field. She wasn't eager to feel overlooked and ignored, but she couldn't leave her family hanging.

"I better get back," she said, and James led her back down the hallway to the front door.

Then, a soft shuffle came from down the hallway. Evelyn turned, surprised to see a woman emerging from a shadowed doorway, moving slowly but with the grace of someone accustomed to being noticed. Her hair was dark and wavy, spilling over her shoulders, and her dress—though simple—seemed to accentuate her every movement. She looked young, younger than Evelyn by a few years, and her smile was radiant as she approached.

"Oh! We have company," the woman said, her hand resting on her belly, her other hand outstretched in greeting. Evelyn saw then that she was pregnant. Her stomach gently curved beneath her dress, and she felt a strange flutter in her own chest.

"I'm Margaret Thompson," she said warmly, her voice soft but full of life. "You must be...?"

"Evelyn Harris," she managed, extending her own hand, though suddenly the warmth she'd felt with James seemed to drain from her. She glanced between James and his wife, feeling the heat rise in her cheeks. "I—I live just down the road. I came by to bring some fresh-baked bread."

Margaret beamed and placed a gentle hand on Evelyn's arm. "Oh, that's so thoughtful. I'm eating for two, so I can't wait to have a slice."

Evelyn forced a small smile, watching as James placed a protective hand on his wife's shoulder, drawing her close. The casual intimacy between them was like a splash of cold water. They were so at ease with one another, a picture of comfort and familiarity she suddenly felt she had no place in.

Margaret looked down at her belly, rubbing it in gentle, rhythmic circles. "This little one—Henry or Helen, depending on who you ask—seems to love food and naps as much as I do. I'm sorry I wasn't awake when you first arrived."

Evelyn laughed politely, though it was thinner now, almost brittle. She felt the edges of her smile tightening, the cheerfulness fading. How foolish she felt now, seeing Margaret's bright eyes and soft laugh, her radiance filling the room in a way that made Evelyn feel almost invisible.

"I understand the need to rest," Evelyn assured her new neighbor, reaching back for the door handle and feeling the coolness of the metal beneath her hand. "I suppose I should be on my way. I didn't mean to intrude."

Margaret tilted her head, her smile unfaltering, her eyes warm. "Oh, no, it's so lovely to meet you. Please, stop by again—perhaps when the baby arrives, and you can help me convince James that Helen is the perfect name."

James laughed, giving his wife a playful nudge. "Let's not make her pick sides just yet."

Evelyn smiled, though it was strained, her heart tightening as she nodded and opened the door. "Well, I'll leave you two to it, then. It was lovely to meet you, Margaret. And James, thank you for... for everything."

James caught her gaze for a fraction of a second, and in that fleeting moment, she thought she saw something in his eyes—a hint of shared understanding, perhaps, or maybe regret. But it was gone in an instant, replaced by a polite smile.

"Anytime, Evelyn," he said quietly. "Please, don't be a stranger."

She managed a last smile, stepping out into the humid air, her heart heavy and tangled. As she walked down the long, winding path back toward her own land, she let the laughter from earlier fade into the quiet. The stillness of the fields settled over her—a reminder of what was hers and what was not.

***

Two Sundays later, when Margaret and James Thompson finally came to church, it was as if a current buzzed through the small congregation. Evelyn tried to focus on the hymnal in her hands, but her mind wandered as the murmurs grew louder.

After the service, Evelyn busied herself with collecting Seth's small Bible, fussing over his coat buttons, and adjusting her own hat. But it wasn't long before she felt a soft hand touch her shoulder.

"Evelyn, it's so lovely to see you," came a light, friendly voice. She looked up to see Margaret's open, eager face framed by the delicate lace of her Sunday hat.

"Likewise, Mrs. Thompson," Evelyn replied, taking Margaret's hand. She tried to mask her surprise with politeness.

"Oh, call me Margaret, please," she said with a small laugh. "Everyone does."

Evelyn nodded, and for a moment, they simply stood together in the shuffle of people filing out of the pews. Margaret kept her hand on Evelyn's arm as though they were already close friends, her eyes softening as they lingered on Evelyn's son.

"And who is this handsome young man?" Margaret asked warmly, kneeling a little to look the boy in the eyes.

"Seth," he replied bashfully.

James approached, his eyes catching Evelyn's with a hint of that reserved smile she remembered. "We're glad to finally be here," he said. "Sorry it took us so long. The unpacking has been..." He shrugged, smiling at his wife.

"Endless," Margaret finished with a laugh, leaning toward him.

Seeing the two of them together—James' steady, familiar presence beside Margaret's lively beauty—left Evelyn feeling strangely off-balance. She could still picture James as she'd seen him from the kitchen window, standing at the edge of his fields, fixing a wheel on his cart.

"Evelyn," Margaret murmured, "I was wondering if you'd like to come by sometime. We're neighbors, after all, and I could use a little help figuring out what to plant in that unruly patch of land by the road. I'd love to hear your thoughts."

Evelyn hesitated, feeling her face flush. "Oh, well... I'd be glad to help however I can," she replied, her voice light. "You might have more luck with Mr. Keller down the road, but I'd be happy to take a look."

Margaret's face brightened, her hand still resting lightly on James's arm. "Perfect. I'll count on it, then."

Evelyn nodded, managing a warm smile as the two of them moved on, greeting the next group of curious onlookers. As she watched them go, Evelyn felt something tighten in her chest. The sight of Margaret's hand wrapped around James's elbow, of her head leaning just so toward him, stayed with her.

Chapter Five

The First Steps Toward Love

The June sun poured over the fields in long, honey-colored ribbons, and Evelyn shaded her eyes as she worked her way through rows of corn, pulling out stubborn weeds by their roots. Her hands were calloused, her fingers rough, but that day, they felt strangely soft, as if her heart, and not her hands, was wrapped in something tender and fragile.

Across the way, just beyond the tree line separating her land from James Thompson's, she saw him—bent over his own row, sleeves rolled to his elbows, exposing the browned skin of his forearms. Evelyn paused, letting her gaze linger on his silhouette as he wiped his brow and stretched his back, his eyes catching hers in the distance. He waved, a small, casual flick of his wrist. Evelyn hesitated, then raised her hand, a warm flush creeping up her neck.

They'd exchanged hellos, brief waves, and polite nods since he'd moved in. At church or in town, she'd seen him with his wife, whispering quietly between themselves. Though she knew he was married, and she was married herself, Evelyn had started to see James in a different light. She caught herself thinking of him at odd times, in the early dawn when the house lay quiet, or in those deep evening hours when Thomas snored in the room beside hers, a rhythm as predictable and permanent as the hills themselves.

She shook her head, willing the thoughts away. But they returned, a whisper, a warmth, something soft and persistent. Schoolgirl foolishness, she told herself firmly, clamping her lips tight as she knelt back down in the dirt. A childish thing to be distracted by the wave of a hand or the kind tilt of a man's eyes.

But later that day, as she walked up the road carrying a basket of eggs to trade with Mrs. Tate, Evelyn felt her heart skip when she heard footsteps behind her. She turned, catching sight of James strolling up the path, his hat in his hand and a polite nod ready.

"Good afternoon, Evelyn," he greeted her with that gentle, slow drawl that seemed to settle in the air between them.

"Good afternoon, James," she replied, her voice soft, her hand tightening on the handle of the basket. They walked in silence for a few paces, the warm wind rustling the tall grass by the roadside.

"Everything all right on your side of the field?" he asked, his tone casual but his gaze resting intently on her.

"Oh, yes," she answered quickly, keeping her gaze fixed straight ahead. "The soil's been good this year. And yourself?"

"Much the same," he replied. "Just trying to keep up, I suppose."

Evelyn nodded, feeling her cheeks warm. Her fingers trembled slightly around the basket handle. The air between them felt thick as if something had shifted—something she hadn't meant to reveal. She offered a small smile, but as her gaze met his, she quickly turned away, her heart beating in quiet alarm.

"Good day, James," she murmured, a quiet urgency coloring her tone as she hurried ahead, her breath unsteady.

As she turned down the lane and made her way to the Tate farm, Evelyn realized that part of her felt as alive as it did foolish, as real as it was fleeting.

A schoolgirl crush, she told herself again, her voice faint and thin against the hum of cicadas. She tried to will the thought away, but it nestled there, small and stubborn, buried just deep enough to grow.

***

The early June air drifted through the open farmhouse kitchen window, carrying the earthy scent of plowed fields and wild honeysuckle. Evelyn stood by the sink, hands deep in soapy water, washing the same cup for the third time. Her gaze drifted out to the patchwork of farmland stretching toward the tree-lined road, where the fence between their property and the Thompsons' stood barely visible, almost swallowed by the tall grass.

She could still hear James's voice from yesterday afternoon, deep and even, asking about the spring rains as they met by the fence. It was an ordinary exchange, just a few words about the weather and soil, yet the warmth of his eyes stayed with her. She had felt her face flush when he'd complimented her garden, her pulse quickening despite herself.

The sharp clatter of silverware in the basin jolted her. Evelyn glanced over her shoulder, worried Thomas might have heard. But he was in the barn, repairing the plow as he had been all morning, unaware of her restless mind. Lately, their words had grown fewer, thinner. Their conversations were woven of practicalities—whether the milk cow needed to be sold, how much to put by for the new tractor part, what to do about the persimmons overtaking the south field. Thomas worked hard, she knew, without ever questioning the back-breaking grind of it all. And she had tried to be the wife he deserved: dependable, loyal, reliable as rain.

But James...

She caught herself smiling, a small tug at the corner of her mouth, and dropped the dish back into the water, splashing her apron. There was something shameful in her heart's betrayals but something thrilling too. She thought of how he had looked at her yesterday, and her chest tightened in a way that was warm and guilty all at once. The very act of thinking his name felt like a small rebellion, a secret tucked beneath her apron.

The creak of the kitchen door broke the quiet, and Thomas's heavy boots thudded over the floor. Evelyn's hands froze in the water as he came up behind her, brushing his rough hand across her back in a familiar, unthinking way.

"Dinner ready soon?" he asked, his voice tired.

"Yes," she said quickly, feeling the weight of the question land between them. "Just a bit more to finish up."

She felt his hand rest on her shoulder, the weight of his presence steady and familiar, but she found herself imagining a different touch, a different warmth. She scolded herself for it, hating the ache that had settled in her chest. She glanced at Thomas, taking in his worn shirt and tired face, softened by the light filtering through the window. He had loved her since they were young, standing by her through thick and thin. He deserved her loyalty, her love—if love could be chosen.

When she turned back to the dishes, her eyes wandered once more toward the road where the fence line disappeared into the trees. She wondered if James might ride by on his tractor this afternoon, wondered if he might stop and wave or even just tip his hat. That thought alone was enough to keep her cheeks flushed, and she scrubbed the dishes harder, as if to scour away the memories.

***

The sun had dipped low behind the rolling hills, casting long shadows across the yard as Evelyn worked her way through the chores. The chickens had been fed, the butter churned, and the last of the laundry hung on the line to dry. Still, she found herself lingering in the barn, pretending to straighten the tools that hung neatly along the walls. Her hands moved methodically, but her thoughts were far from the tasks at hand.

She couldn't stop thinking about James. She had seen him earlier that morning, down by the fence, tending to the horses. Just a few words exchanged, nothing more. But those words had carried a weight that lingered in her chest, heavy and unsettling. Her heart still fluttered at the memory of his voice, the quiet way he asked after the crops, the brief, unspoken connection in the way his eyes met hers.

Evelyn clenched her jaw and forced her thoughts back to the barn, running her fingers along the smooth wood of the pitchfork handle, as if the simple motion could erase the image of him. It's just a passing thought, she told herself. Just a neighbor, nothing more. She shook her head, dismissing the flutter in her chest as something fleeting, silly even.

But deep down, she knew it wasn't that simple. It had started with those fleeting glances, the way his presence seemed to fill the spaces around her when they spoke. At first, she thought it was nothing—just a friendly exchange between neighbors, the kind she'd had a hundred times before. But this... this felt different. She felt something stir inside her—something she hadn't felt in years.

It wasn't like the early days with Thomas. That had been a steady, solid love built on trust and familiarity. But with James, it was sharper, more fragile, like the first taste of something sweet after a long drought. It reminded her of the schoolgirl crush she'd had before she'd married

Thomas, when the flutter of a boy's attention had made her cheeks pink with excitement.

The thought made her feel guilty, as if she were betraying something sacred. You're a grown woman, she scolded herself. You've been married for nearly fifteen years. You have a family. You don't have the luxury of such foolishness anymore. But the guilt was always followed by a pang of longing, a hunger she hadn't known existed in so long.

Evelyn wiped a hand across her forehead, feeling the dampness of sweat mixed with the faint ache in her heart. She thought of Thomas, working in the fields. He was solid and dependable, but somehow, that was all he was now. Dependable. He had become a fixture in her life, like the walls of this house. She loved him, yes, but the warmth she had once felt in his presence had slowly faded, like the embers of a fire that had burned down to nothing more than ash.

James was different. He was still a question, an unknown that stirred something inside her. And that uncertainty, that possibility, was a spark she hadn't realized she missed until now.

"Stop it," she muttered. She set the pitchfork down, the scraping sound echoing too loudly in the silence. She needed to stop this before it went any further.

But deep in her chest, where the fire of possibility burned just beneath her ribs, she knew she couldn't. The thought of him had lodged itself deep in her heart, and no matter how hard she tried, she couldn't push it out.

***

The next Sunday at church, Evelyn sat stiffly on the worn wooden pew, her fingers twisting the edge of her hymnal, the words of the psalm blurring in her mind. The heavy scent of candle wax and polished wood clung to the air, mingling with the musty smell of old books from the rows of shelves near the altar. She had always enjoyed church, a place of routine, of stillness. But today, there was an unease that she couldn't shake.

Her gaze drifted, almost involuntarily, toward the far side of the church where James sat with his head bowed, his hands folded neatly in front of him. The soft light filtering through the stained glass painted patches of color across his dark suit. She had never noticed how fine the lines of his jaw looked in the sunlight or how his shoulders, though stooped in prayer, held a quiet strength. A quiet strength that made her heart lurch.

For a moment, the world seemed to fall away. The rustling of the congregation's hymnal pages, the murmured prayers, the faint creak of the pews, all faded to a distant hum. There was only James across the aisle, so near and yet so far. Her chest tightened. She quickly looked down at her lap, biting her lower lip, willing herself to focus.

But then, her eyes darted back to him against her better judgment. James lifted his head slightly, his gaze flicking to hers with the sharpness of someone who had been aware of her every move. Their eyes met for the briefest of moments, an unspoken understanding passing between them. And then, without breaking his steady gaze, he gave her a small, fleeting smile—so subtle, so laden with meaning, that it seemed to fill the entire space between them. A smile that lingered like a secret shared only between the two of them.

Evelyn's breath caught in her throat. She didn't know whether to look away or hold his gaze, but the moment was shattered by the hand Margaret placed gently on James's forearm. He immediately turned his smile to his wife, and Evelyn quickly looked back to the front of the church, forcing herself to focus on the hymn being sung. The moment between her and James hung in the air, lingering like a secret.

And for the first time, Evelyn wasn't sure if it was one she wanted to keep.

***

The kitchen smelled of fresh bread, a comforting scent that usually made Evelyn feel at ease. But today, as she folded the dough with quick, purposeful movements, her thoughts churned. She could hear the muffled sound of Thomas's boots shuffling across the porch outside, his heavy tread as familiar as the rhythm of her own heart. He was back from the fields, and with him, the weight of another long day's labor.

Evelyn slid the dough into the baking pan, her hands stiff from the work, but her mind was far from the task. She glanced toward the window, where Thomas was settling into his chair at the table, his long legs sprawled out in front of him, looking every bit the man who worked himself ragged for the land.

She wiped her hands on her apron and took a deep breath before crossing the room. "Thomas, we need to talk."

He didn't lift his eyes from the paper he was reading. "There's nothing to talk about. Just trying to keep up with the harvest."

"I'm not talking about the harvest," Evelyn said, her voice sharper than she intended. She took the seat opposite him, a small frown tugging at her lips. "I've been thinking... about the farm. The land."

Thomas sighed but didn't look up. He folded the paper in half and set it down. "Not this again."

"We're running low on savings," she continued, pressing on despite his disinterest. "The Depression's only getting worse, Thomas. Maybe we should sell an acre or two. We could get by for a while, maybe even make sure Seth's future's a little more secure." She didn't add that she'd been losing sleep over the thought of how quickly the money would run out. The world outside the farm felt like it was crumbling, but in the heart of their home, it seemed like it was just the two of them, stranded in a life that felt too heavy to hold.

Thomas leaned back, his hands resting on his knees, the muscles in his arms taut beneath his shirtsleeves. He stared at her as though the suggestion was something she'd pulled out of the air. "We've never sold a damn acre. And I'm not about to start now." His voice was steady, but there was a coldness to it that Evelyn hadn't expected.

"I know the land means everything to you," she said quietly, her gaze drifting to the window where the horizon met the dirt road that led to James's farm. "It means a lot to me, too. It's my family's. But we can't live on pride alone. We need to be practical. We can't just keep working the soil like nothing's changing. I don't want to lose everything. Everything we've built."

His jaw tightened, and she saw his fingers twitch at his sides. But when he spoke, his voice was thick with something else—resentment, maybe, or just exhaustion. "I'll work harder, Evelyn. I always have. I don't need to sell the land. We've got plenty to get by. The crops will do better this year, you'll see."

The words stung, not because they weren't true—she knew how hard he worked—but because of the dismissive ease with which he said them. He had an answer for everything, and yet it never seemed to make the weight of their reality any lighter. She watched him, the faint lines of age deepening around his eyes, the stoop of his shoulders from years of bending over the fields. She didn't know when it had started, but the distance between them had only grown wider.

"I don't want you to work harder, Thomas. I want you to be here." She said it before she could stop herself, the words slipping out like a confession. "I want you to be with me. With Seth."

He paused, a long stretch of silence between them. Then he sighed, standing up abruptly and brushing past her, his shirt sleeves brushing against the back of her hand as he moved to the door. "I'll be out in the fields again tomorrow morning. I've got work to do."

Evelyn sat there, her hands clasped in her lap, watching him leave. A pit formed in her stomach as she looked at the table where the bread dough had risen, waiting to be baked. The farm was so much more than land to her—it was family, it was history, it was the lifeblood of everything she'd known. But right now, she didn't know if she wanted it anymore.

The door closed behind him with a quiet thud, and Evelyn was left alone in the stillness, the weight of the farm pressing in on her chest.

Chapter Six

Dear James

July 1932

Dear James,

Writing this letter feels strange, even wrong, yet I find myself here, pen in hand, driven by a restlessness I don't know how to quiet. I'm not certain what I aim to accomplish by putting these words to paper; after all, it's not as if I could ever pass this letter on to you. I wouldn't know how to look you in the eye again if I did. But there are things I feel—things that are impossible to say out loud—that fill my heart and mind to bursting. So here I am, speaking to you in the only way I know how.

There have been moments, small ones that might seem trivial to an outsider, that stay with me long after they pass. Do you remember when I handed you that bag of flour at the market last month? Your fingers brushed mine, just for an instant. Such a simple touch, but my heart quickened as if I were a girl again. I lingered on the memory of that touch for days afterward, despite knowing how ridiculous that sounds.

Then, there are the times I catch you looking at me, like last Sunday at church. I felt your gaze on me as though it were a gentle hand, warm and steady, and for a second, I almost turned to meet it. But I couldn't. The preacher's voice was echoing through the rafters, and Thomas sat just a few inches away, his shoulder brushing against mine. Your own wife was beside you, yet the thought of your eyes on me made it hard to concentrate on anything but the ache stirring in my chest.

I feel as if I'm betraying something sacred by thinking of you like this. I've spent nearly all my life being the kind of woman I'm expected to be: a good wife, a good neighbor, and, above all, a quiet and dutiful presence. I'm meant to feel whole in my marriage and content with my duties. But sometimes, when I'm alone, I catch myself wondering what it would be like to feel something more.

You make me wonder, James. I find myself thinking of you in those moments when the house is silent, when Thomas is away in the fields, and Seth is at school. I imagine your laugh, your voice, the way you smile as though you're hiding a secret. I don't think you realize the kindness you show people or how rare it is. I've grown used to glances full of judgment, whispers that weigh heavy with what others expect of me. But you look at me in a way that reminds me of who I was before I was ever someone's wife.

I know that thinking this way is dangerous, especially here, where eyes and ears are everywhere. But my heart aches for something I can't name, and each day, it grows a little harder to silence it. I can't tell if I write this letter hoping to banish these feelings or to give them a voice. All I know is that these words—this letter—are the closest I'll ever come to telling you how you make me feel.

Perhaps I'll burn this letter the moment it's finished. Perhaps I'll keep it tucked away, unread, for the rest of my days. Either way, I don't expect you'll ever see it.

But I needed to say it, if only to myself: these feelings are real, as real as the earth beneath my feet and the sky over my head. And no matter what I do, they don't seem to fade.

Yours in a way I cannot fully understand,

Evelyn

Chapter Seven

The Pain of Separation

The late summer air held a softness that carried through the rolling Tennessee hills, draping the fields in warmth as Evelyn walked down Willow Branch Road. She held a basket with a Mason jar of lemonade inside, her head tilted down as the familiar path guided her and her thoughts drifted. She hadn't seen James in days, but she knew his routine well enough to guess he'd be mending fences along the eastern edge of his property.

Sure enough, as she neared the wooden stile, she saw him—broad-shouldered and bent over, hands steady as he worked. He straightened at the sound of her footsteps, brushing his hands on his worn trousers. His hat shadowed his face, but Evelyn could see the grin tugging at his mouth.

"Well now, what's the occasion?" he asked, his drawl slow and warm.

"Just thought I'd bring over a little something," she replied, lifting the basket. "It's no special occasion, really."

He took the basket from her hands, his fingers grazing hers. "Thank you, Evelyn. You know, you're about the only neighbor who'd bother to bring anything these days. Seems like no baby news, no interest." His laughter fell flat, and the exhaustion on his face was clear.

She shrugged, settling against the fence, her fingers trailing along the rough wood. " I figured you could use some company."

They fell into an easy silence as he sipped the lemonade straight from the jar, broken only by the sounds of cicadas and distant lowing cattle. James turned to her, his gaze steady, the warmth in his eyes mingling with something else she couldn't quite name.

"Can I say something without soundin' ungrateful?" he asked, glancing toward the sun dipping low behind the hills.

"Go on," she replied, smiling. "I've got thick skin."

James chuckled, pulling off his hat to rub at the back of his neck. "Folks around here... they'll show up for a barn dance, or a service, or if someone's born or buried. But they won't say a word about what's between all that."

Evelyn nodded slowly, understanding more than she could say. "They'll watch from afar but not get too close," she murmured. "I know that feeling too."

"And I guess..." He trailed off, eyes flicking to the side as though embarrassed. "I guess sometimes I just get plain tired of the rudeness of it."

She studied his face, softened in the twilight. "Well, James, you're not alone today," she said softly. "We both have our frustrations, don't we?"

He turned to her, eyebrows raised. "Oh? Do tell, Mrs. Harris."

She laughed, tucking a loose strand of hair behind her ear. "It's nothin' you haven't heard before. Most days, I feel like a bird in a too-small cage. Can't open my mouth without wonderin' what

Thomas will think, or what Seth will need. I love them both dear-
ly—don't mistake me—but sometimes..." She sighed, letting the
thought linger.

James studied her in silence, a kindness in his gaze that felt both
comforting and dangerous. "Sometimes," he said, echoing her words
softly, "it's just nice to talk to someone who understands."

They shared a smile, and for a moment, Evelyn felt as if a weight had
lifted. Here, out of earshot of everyone else, she could be herself. No
need for pretense.

"You know," James said, leaning back against the fence post beside
her, "when we first moved in, folks were kind enough for a while.
Brought casseroles and sat with us. But it's like you said—they kept
their distance once they thought they knew us. Like they just wanted
some new gossip."

Evelyn's heart softened as she looked at him, the vulnerability in his
eyes startling yet familiar. "People see what they want to see," she said,
voice barely a whisper.

He nodded, his hand reaching to brush a speck of dust from her
shoulder. "Sometimes I think you're the only person who's honest
around here, Evelyn."

The silence that followed felt thick with words they dared not say.
Evelyn felt her breath catch as she met his gaze, searching for words
that wouldn't come. How could she talk to this man about honesty
when she was harboring such secret feelings for him? Feelings for him
instead of her husband? Finally, she offered a small smile, resting her
hand briefly atop his on the fence post. "Well, James, I suppose that
makes two of us."

They stood there as the sun dipped toward the horizon, bound
by something unspoken but undeniably real, aware of how wrong it

might look if anyone saw them. But in that moment, they were alone, two kindred souls sharing a rare and precious understanding.

***

Days later, the late afternoon sun slanted through the willow trees, casting dappled light on the quiet path Evelyn and James walked together. It was only half a mile from the market back to her farm, a short walk she'd made countless times on her own or with Seth skipping ahead. But today, it was just the two of them, and Evelyn felt every quiet step, every light breeze stirring the air between them.

"Well, you sure showed Mrs. Winfield how a pie crust should be made today," James said, his voice laced with amusement. "Poor woman looked ready to defend her entire family recipe collection after you gave her that tip on flour."

Evelyn chuckled, imagining the tight-lipped shock on Mrs. Winfield's face. "She's a proud one, I'll give her that. But it wouldn't hurt her to use less lard in her dough. She'd thank me if she'd try it."

"Oh, she'd thank you, alright," James said, a hint of teasing in his tone. "Probably with a note pinned to a basket of burnt biscuits."

She laughed, and he joined her, their laughter ringing like a brief song. But the laughter faded as they slowed at the Willow Branch road bend separating their houses.

Evelyn cleared her throat, forcing herself to look at the sunlit trees rather than him. "Well, it's nice, isn't it? Having someone to talk to about things. Small things that don't matter."

James took a breath, glancing toward the overgrown branches that framed their little pocket of shade. "I never realized how much difference that can make," he said softly. "Talking to you—it makes a hard day a lot less hard. Managing everything on the farm is one thing, but also handling everything in the house with Margaret on bed rest... it's taxing."

She felt her heart stumble, a tiny beat too fast. She tried to hear only the compliment, not the mention of his wife. "We... we should be careful, though, James. This town watches, even when it doesn't mean to. It doesn't take much to set off the gossip, and I don't want them to think something is happening when it isn't."

He nodded, looking down at the dust gathering around his boots. "I know. I worry about that too." He hesitated, his voice quiet. "Do you think... maybe we ought not to walk together? Not like this."

The suggestion felt like a blow, though she'd been the one to raise the issue. "I suppose it'd be sensible. We both have our families to think about."

They fell silent, both staring at the dusty ground. A bird chirped somewhere in the branches above, oblivious to their struggle.

"But I'd miss it," he murmured after a moment, the words coming out in a hushed confession. He didn't look at her as he spoke, his gaze fixed somewhere past the trees. "Talking like this. Laughing like this."

Her heart thudded louder, and she felt a warmth creep into her cheeks. She didn't answer right away, afraid her voice might betray her.

"I would too," she whispered finally, her eyes drifting up to meet his. She wanted to hold that moment, to linger in the way he looked at her, as though she were someone worth remembering, someone he couldn't bear to lose.

They stood there, close enough to feel the pull between them, that invisible line tethering her heart to his. She knew it was wrong, yet standing there with him felt as if the world had folded in on itself, leaving only them.

"Maybe," she said, forcing herself to smile, "we should try and be a little more distant for a while. For our families' sake, at least."

He nodded slowly. "That might be best."

They lingered another beat before she stepped back, the distance feeling like a chasm already. She nodded, turned, and began walking the remaining steps toward her farm, each footfall echoing the ache of their unspoken words. As she reached the path to her house, she glanced back. He stood there watching, a quiet shadow against the sunlit road, as though he, too, couldn't quite let go.

She forced a smile, hoping he couldn't see the longing she felt, and continued on her way home, telling herself that this would be the last time—though deep down, she wasn't sure she could keep such a promise.

***

Evelyn felt the quiet press in around her as she went about her chores, the ache of the empty spaces where James's voice used to fill the silence almost unbearable. She knew the decision had been right. Necessary. The cost of being careless was too steep, the risks too great. But still, she missed the way he understood her, how easily conversation flowed when they spoke about books or the world outside this town, a world neither of them would ever truly know.

One morning, as she gathered eggs from the henhouse, she felt a shadow stretch across her field. Instinctively, she looked up, her heart quickening. It was James, standing just across the fence line, his hand raised in a wave. The sight of him there, so close yet unreachable, made her chest tighten.

They locked eyes for a brief moment, and she saw something in his expression—a question, maybe, or a longing that mirrored her own. She glanced down quickly, feeling the blush rise in her cheeks, but when she looked up, he hadn't moved.

That evening, Evelyn found herself walking to the very edge of her land, pausing at the fence line. She didn't dare go further, but she lingered, hoping he might appear on the other side. The wind carried the faint scent of pine, and she closed her eyes, listening to the quiet, hoping it might bring his footsteps along with it.

The days wore on, and her resolve weakened with each glance across the fields. On Saturday, she saw him in town by the general store, loading flour into the back of his wagon. Their eyes met, a spark of recognition, and he nodded, a small gesture but one that said so much. It was the briefest of acknowledgments, yet it sent warmth through her.

And then, on a foggy morning just before dawn, she spotted him on the far side of the pasture, closer to her land than he had any right to be. He moved slowly as though pretending to inspect the fence posts or scout for stray cattle. She watched him from her kitchen window, torn between calling out and staying hidden, caught in the thrill and danger of these tiny rebellions.

She knew it couldn't go on; these stolen glances and silent promises left unspoken. But every time he looked her way, every wave, every step nearer her land—it was like the thread of something inevitable pulling them closer, a bond that distance couldn't sever.

***

The emptiness settled around Evelyn, especially when she was in the kitchen, filling every corner of the quiet room where she spent most of her time. She leaned back against the doorway, feeling a wave of something she couldn't quite name. Loneliness, maybe, but deeper, like a hole she'd only just discovered in the middle of her heart.

The house had a stillness that had become familiar over the past months. Thomas slept in their boy's room, saying it was more practical with the early mornings and the work piling up. Evelyn hadn't argued; she understood the demands of the farm. She even told herself that it was sensible. But the quiet nights, with no warmth beside her, had changed something in her, left her feeling hollow. She had never expected her marriage to look like this, but she didn't know how to make it better. Especially not when her thoughts were still so consumed by someone else. Who was she to ask her husband to come back to their marital bed when it wasn't him who lived in her daydreams?

She walked slowly into the small parlor, her hand grazing over the worn fabric of the armchair as she moved. Her fingers lingered, tracing old stains, the subtle fraying at the edges. She tried to shake off the thoughts that seemed to cling to her, but her mind drifted, unwillingly as always, to James. To the moments at the fence, the few stolen glances, the quiet nods exchanged across the fields. A spark of something bright, alive, where her own house felt shadowed and dull.

She let herself imagine, just for a moment, what it might feel like if things were different. What if she could talk to James the way they did in those rare, fleeting moments—about everything and nothing, things Thomas would never take the time to understand? She pressed her lips together, ashamed at the thought, but her heart pulled all the same, like a flower bending toward sunlight.

The farm life she'd been born into had always come with expectations and responsibilities. And she'd been good, hadn't she? Dutiful. She had married the man her parents thought best, had managed the house, cared for Seth, done her share on the farm without a single complaint. And yet, here she was, yearning for something that wasn't hers to have, something that felt as dangerous as it was inevitable.

Evelyn sank into the armchair and covered her face with her hands. She inhaled deeply, fighting the tears that pricked at her eyes. What was this ache? This gnawing emptiness that James somehow seemed to fill without even meaning to?

She dropped her hands and stared across the room, her gaze lingering on the old clock that ticked steadily against the wall. She thought of her few precious moments with him—the warmth in his voice, the way he seemed to understand things she never needed to explain. In those moments, she felt seen, even cherished, in a way that had slipped away over time with Thomas.

But could she risk it? All she had built here, all she had fought to hold together, could be undone in an instant. And the cost—she couldn't bear to think of what it might do to Seth, to Thomas, to the fragile life they had patched together.

She squeezed her eyes shut, willing herself to remember that loneliness was a small price to pay for the life she was meant to lead, the life her family needed her to keep.

Chapter Eight

The Tragic Loss

E velyn's hands trembled as she set down the bucket, her heart hammering against her ribs in an unfamiliar, almost painful way. The news had reached her barely an hour ago—Margaret Thompson was in labor, and something had gone terribly wrong.

She didn't dare approach the Thompsons' house. Some other neighbors were gathered already, murmuring in quiet circles along the edge of the road. Instead, Evelyn stood just outside her barn, her eyes fixed on the darkening path winding through the trees that led up to their house. She couldn't stop imagining James pacing inside, alone and helpless.

Her fingers gripped her shawl tightly as she sank onto an overturned bucket, her breathing shallow. She hated the helplessness in her bones, as if her body recognized the shadow that now threatened the house across the way. Evelyn's gaze fell on the road, her mind reaching for some comforting prayer, but none came. It seemed wrong to wish for relief, knowing such relief would now come at the most terrible cost.

Sometime later, just as dusk settled its heavy purple cloak across the horizon, she saw a figure moving down the road. It was Mrs. Walker, her shoulders bent under a shawl. Evelyn's breath caught in her throat; Mrs. Walker had been one of the midwives. If she was leaving...

A bitter chill ran down Evelyn's spine. She rose to her feet, her body taut as a string, watching Mrs. Walker move with the slow, defeated shuffle of someone who has left all hope behind.

She didn't want to ask. But she couldn't stop herself.

"Mrs. Walker," she called, her voice barely above a whisper.

The older woman stopped, turning to Evelyn with tired eyes that said more than words ever could.

"They...they're gone, Evelyn," Mrs. Walker murmured, her voice thick. "Both of 'em. Margaret—she didn't make it. The baby, well, he held on a little longer, but it wasn't enough. James..." She looked away, her voice falling to a hush. "He's in pieces, that poor man."

Evelyn pressed a hand to her mouth, the enormity of the loss sinking into her like stones. The baby—the child Margaret had been waiting so long to hold, the one she had talked about with such hope—gone. And Margaret, too, her bright laughter, the kindness in her eyes, all swept away in a single, brutal night. Every unkind thought Evelyn had ever thought about Margaret, wishing herself as James's wife instead, felt like it was stabbing her in the gut, riddling her with grief that she knew couldn't compare to what James was feeling now. But she had to live with those thoughts now.

A hollow ache settled in Evelyn's chest as she watched Mrs. Walker continue down the path, her steps slow and heavy. When she disappeared from view, Evelyn sank to her knees beside the barn, the damp earth cold against her skin. She wanted to cry but felt as though her tears had frozen somewhere deep inside. All she could feel was the weight of James's loss pressing down on her, filling her with an ache that no prayer could touch.

In her mind, she pictured James, his head in his hands, alone in that dark, empty house. She pictured the nursery Margaret had lovingly prepared, the tiny cradle that would remain empty. The silence that would now haunt him every night.

For a long moment, Evelyn remained there, kneeling in the cold grass, clutching her shawl as the night deepened around her. She wasn't family; she wasn't the one who belonged by his side in this grief. But she could feel it all the same, as though his sorrow had found a way to reach her across the fields, settling into her bones, making itself a part of her.

At last, Evelyn rose, wiping her hands against her skirt. She stared down the road that led to the Thompsons' house, hesitating. She longed to go to him, to tell him she understood, that he wasn't alone in this silent, awful night. But she knew she couldn't. Not now.

Instead, Evelyn turned back toward her own house, feeling the weight of his grief settle over her like the night itself, and whispered a soft, broken prayer for them all.

***

Evelyn sat at the kitchen table, the stove's warmth struggling to chase the chill that had settled in her bones. She'd been waiting all morning for something to happen, though she didn't know what—the minutes dragging by with unbearable slowness. The soft murmur of voices in the yard outside faded in and out, muffled by the thick walls of the house. She had heard the horses and the doctor's truck arrive not long after she spoke to Mrs. Walker. After that, silence.

The air inside Evelyn's lungs felt tight, as if something in her chest had been crushed. Margaret was gone, and though Evelyn had always kept her distance, this was the kind of grief that didn't just stay with the person it belonged to. It was something shared.

She forced herself to walk across the now-empty yard and approach the back of her neighbor's house. She hesitated at the door but ignored her second thoughts and pulled open the screen door, which had been left unlatched by someone who had been in and out of the house that day.

She walked past the shadowy hallway to the room where James must have been waiting all morning. His face was ashen, his hands trembling as he held a bundle of faded cloth—an empty baby blanket, Evelyn could see as she stepped into the room.

James's eyes were red from crying; his shoulders slumped with the weight of a grief that seemed to have crushed him entirely. Evelyn's throat tightened, her heart stuttering in her chest.

"James?" she whispered, stepping closer to him.

He didn't look up right away. His gaze was locked on the baby blanket, his fingers grazing gently over the cloth. It took a moment before he lifted his eyes, his face twisted in a mixture of sorrow and disbelief.

"He's gone," James murmured, the words thick with grief. "But I held him. I held Henry, Evelyn."

Evelyn nodded, her heart aching for him in a way she couldn't quite explain. She walked closer, her eyes drawn to the blanket in his arms.

"I never thought it would feel like this," he said, his voice breaking. "I never thought I'd have a child and lose him in the same breath."

Evelyn couldn't speak for a moment. Her chest tightened, and all she could do was watch as James looked down at his son's unused blanket, his face a mask of sorrow.

"You named him Henry?" she asked softly, her voice a whisper in the stillness.

He nodded slowly, his hands clutching the blanket a little tighter. "Margaret wanted him to be Henry. She spoke about it so often. I wanted to keep that for her, at least. Henry." His voice cracked, and he blinked rapidly as if trying to stave off tears.

Evelyn's gaze softened as she watched him. She wasn't sure what she could say, how she could make this right, but she knew one thing: James had loved Margaret with a quiet, steadfast love. And this, this loss, was his to carry alone.

For a long time, neither of them spoke. Time passed, yet it stood still in that room.

Finally, James stirred, shifting his position as though the weight of the blanket was too much. He gently handed it to Evelyn, his movements slow and reluctant. She cradled the blanket in her arms, wishing it wasn't empty. For all she had felt for James, all of her silly fantasies of another life, this was never in the mix. She wouldn't wish this on anyone.

"You're a good man, James," Evelyn whispered as she stared down at the blanket. "This loss, it won't change that."

James sank back into the chair, his gaze far away, lost in the sorrow of a love that had never been fully realized. The room was heavy with the grief of a life that had ended far too soon, and as Evelyn stood there, she wondered if James's heart would ever be whole again.

***

Evelyn stood at the edge of the hill, where the wind carried the scent of damp earth and the distant rustle of leaves. The graveside was quiet—the kind of quiet that made her feel as though the world had gone still just for a moment. Her eyes fixed on James, standing alone beside the freshly turned soil. His back was straight, his hands clasped in front of him, but Evelyn knew him well enough to see the tension in the lines of his shoulders, the way his jaw worked beneath the stubble.

The earth had swallowed Margaret and Henry too quickly, too silently, and now James was left with only his grief. She should have been there—she should have gone to him. But instead, she remained where she was, hidden by the trees at the far edge of the cemetery. Her feet felt frozen in place, as though the ground had a claim on her. She longed to walk to him, to put her arms around him, but she couldn't. The unspoken rules of the world between them were too heavy, too binding.

She watched the way he knelt beside the graves, his broad hand brushing over the dirt as if he could touch her again through the earth. His lips moved, but no sound reached her. Evelyn's heart twisted. The sorrow for him—a sorrow she had no right to claim—pushed against the walls of her chest.

His wife and son were both dead before the world could even begin to understand what it had taken from him. And James was left with only pain. She wanted to say something—anything—that might ease his burden, but words seemed too small, too hollow.

James stood slowly as if the weight of the moment might drag him down. He took one last look at the grave and turned toward the road, his face unreadable, as though he had swallowed all the tears that had threatened to spill. Evelyn felt the sudden, sharp sting of tears in her own eyes, but she quickly wiped them away, refusing to let him see them.

In that silent, aching moment, Evelyn felt a strange, intimate connection with him—an understanding that had never existed between her and Thomas, no matter how many years they had shared under the same roof. Thomas could never understand the things she kept buried, the longings she couldn't speak of. But James? James carried grief with him in a way she recognized. It was a grief she knew too well, the kind that shaped everything in its wake.

Evelyn exhaled slowly, her chest tight. She would never cross the distance, never be the comfort he needed. She couldn't. It wasn't proper. She would remain the shadow on the edge of his life, never stepping fully into the light. It was the way of things, the way it had always been. But for just a moment, watching him disappear into the horizon, Evelyn allowed herself the briefest of wishes: that she could have been there for him in some way that didn't hurt them both.

As the sound of his footsteps faded, she stayed rooted to the ground, the ache of it all sinking deep into her bones.

***

James hadn't been the same since Margaret and Henry had passed. Now his brow was always furrowed, the lightness in his eyes replaced by an almost unbearable weight. Evelyn had watched him from the corner of her kitchen window more than once, a silhouette in the fading light, staring into the distance as though the land itself could offer some comfort.

But now, as she stood on the porch that morning, waiting for him to come by, she felt an unsettling pull toward him. It was a pull she'd tried to ignore for months, but it was there now, undeniable and growing.

Evelyn knew she shouldn't feel this way, and yet she did.

Willow Branch Road, the dirt path between their two homes, had always felt like a boundary, a line she had never dared cross too easily, especially now, to visit a man who lived alone. But today, for some reason, it didn't seem so far. When James came into view, his gait slow, his shoulders slumped, she knew—knew without him saying a word—that the life he had once dreamed of had slipped away, as if it had never been his, to begin with.

"James," she called softly, her voice barely rising above the hum of the wind, but he heard her.

His head turned, eyes briefly meeting hers before he lowered them again, a sadness too deep for words in the way his mouth twitched.

He had quickly become a fixture of the land next to hers, but this man—this broken man—seemed like someone else entirely. He nodded in her direction but didn't move closer, not yet.

"I thought you might want company," she said, taking a cautious step toward him. The words felt foreign in her mouth, heavy.

He didn't speak for a long moment. Evelyn watched him closely, the familiar lines of his face now etched with grief. He had lost his wife. He had lost the child he'd imagined raising, teaching to walk and talk, playing in the fields. She could see it in him now—how it filled up every space inside him. How it made him hollow.

"I don't need company," he finally muttered, his voice thick, hoarse. He took a deep breath, exhaling like the weight of his own heart could suffocate him if he didn't. "I'm alone now, so it must be what was intended for me."

Evelyn felt a pang in her chest, a sorrow she had never allowed herself to express, the unspoken bond between them pulsing in the silence. The distance between them wasn't just physical now; it was an ocean of unspoken things, things they both knew but didn't dare acknowledge. Not yet. Not yet.

"Sometimes, things happen for reasons we don't understand," she said, hoping her sentiment didn't sound too pithy. She cleared her throat, but her voice came out barely a whisper. "But it doesn't hurt to have someone nearby, does it?"

He glanced at her then, and for the briefest of moments, there was a flicker of something in his eyes—something like relief, something like regret. But it was gone too quickly for her to grasp. He wasn't ready for it, not now. Still, she remained standing there, waiting, her breath soft in the cold morning air.

The distance between them was still too great. But Evelyn knew, deep down, that it wouldn't always be. One day, this brokenness would somehow find its way into something else—something neither of them had planned or ever wanted to acknowledge. But, for now, there was only silence, the earth beneath her feet and the broken man before her.

And it was enough, for now.

Chapter Nine

Dear Evelyn

November 4, 1932

Dear Evelyn,

I hope this letter finds you well. I cannot express enough how much I appreciate the food you've so kindly brought to my house these past few weeks. The meals have been a great comfort to me during these dark days, and I find it difficult to fully express how much they've meant. The coldness of my kitchen and the emptiness of the house is a bit more bearable, with something warm and nourishing to fill it.

I must confess, it is not just the food itself that I am grateful for—though I will admit the stew you prepared was as good as any I've had, and that bread, well, it has been a rare treat—but it is the thoughtfulness behind it. In your kindness, you have provided me with more than just a meal; you've given me a reminder of human connection, of caring at a time when I have felt very much alone.

Your visits, brief though they are, have brought a small, much-needed light into my life. There are times when it seems as if the weight of everything—Margaret's passing, the loss of Henry and the life he could have had, the hollowness of the days—threatens to consume me. And yet, in those fleeting moments when you stop by, I feel the stirrings of something that has long been absent: peace. There's a quiet comfort in your presence, a sense of familiarity that eases the burden on my heart, even if just for a short while. I suppose I'm grateful for that in a way I can hardly put into words.

I know I must sound terribly ungrateful for dwelling on such personal matters, especially when you have already done so much. But the truth is, your kindness has touched me in a way I hadn't expected. I imagine you might see your visits as nothing more than a small favor, but to me, they have been a reminder that, even in the deepest sorrow, there are still moments of connection to be had. And for that, I will be forever thankful.

I do not wish to make this letter too long or too wordy, but I hope you understand just how much your kindness has meant to me, and I trust you know that it is something I will not soon forget.

Please take care of yourself, Mrs. Harris. I hope the coming weeks bring you peace, as your generosity has brought me.

With respect and gratitude,

James Thompson

Chapter Ten

The Unthinkable

The kitchen smelled of onions and garlic—the hearty scent of stew thick in the air as Evelyn stirred the pot. Her hands moved instinctively, but her mind was elsewhere, trailing over the same thought that had been stirring in her chest for days...

It had been nearly a month since Margaret passed, and Evelyn had only seen James twice since then. The first time, she'd brought a basket of bread, a pie, a tin of preserves. She'd set it on his porch without so much as a word between them, only a nod, and left quickly before her heart could betray her. The second time, just days ago, she had stopped by to drop off more food but stayed to offer a few soft words of comfort. She hadn't meant to stay so long. She had meant only to be kind, but the quiet that fell between them had felt too heavy to leave behind. There was something in his eyes—a kind of sadness she understood and yet something more. She hadn't known what it was then, and she certainly didn't know now.

Her thoughts were interrupted as she wiped her hands on her apron and placed the dish in the oven. It wasn't just kindness this time. It was something else—something that twisted her insides and made her feel both foolish and certain all at once. She was going to see him again, and this time, she would not be able to leave without saying the things she hadn't yet dared to.

It was late afternoon when Evelyn set out, carrying a fresh pot of stew wrapped in a cloth. The day was fading quickly, the air sharp with the hint of winter. The sky was soft and gray, the kind of afternoon when the air felt thick with promises. Evelyn stood on the porch, the basket of food warm against her arm. It wasn't a chore, not this time. She had decided, somewhere between the stove and the back door, that she needed to go. There was something pulling at her, an invisible thread she couldn't ignore. The decision was made before she could talk herself out of it.

She hadn't told Thomas, not that he would have cared. She was used to moving quietly around him, like a shadow that belonged to no one but herself. Their marriage had long since become an arrangement, a quiet understanding between two people who didn't speak of things they both knew to be true. But James—she didn't know what she felt for him, only that her heart raced at the thought of him.

She walked slowly down Willow Branch Road, usually a familiar path, but today it felt unfamiliar, like she was walking into a new world. The bare branches of the trees reached overhead, their skeletal fingers twisting together to form a canopy, shielding the way like a secret passage. The world around her was still, save for the soft rustling of wind through the leaves, the way they always whispered in the quiet of this place. As she walked, the ache in her chest grew, pressing against her ribs like a weight.

Her boots crunched on the frozen dirt as she made her way toward the Thompson house, the overgrown trees looming like silent sentinels around her. The scent of woodsmoke and earth clung to the air as she reached the front door. She hesitated for just a moment, but then she knocked softly, the sound muffled by the old wood. A moment passed before the door creaked open.

James stood there, his face worn, his eyes shadowed in a way she hadn't seen before. The sight of him struck her harder than she expected. He was always so strong, so self-contained, but now his shoulders were slumped, and the edges of his usual stoic expression had softened. The weight of it—the grief, the loneliness—seemed to hang around him, thick as fog.

"Evelyn," he said, his voice rough, like he hadn't spoken in days. "Come in."

She stepped inside, and the warmth of the room was a comfort. The fire crackled in the hearth, casting flickering shadows on the walls. The smell of stew hung in the air, and she set the basket down on the table, pushing a few stray strands of hair behind her ear.

"You've been good to me these past weeks. I don't know what I'd have done without you," he murmured, though his eyes were fixed on the basket, not her. His hands trembled slightly as he reached for it and stepped back to let her inside.

She followed him, trying to steady the wild thumping of her heart. "You've been alone too much, James. Thought you could use a little company and some food to stick to your ribs."

"Will you eat with me?" he asked in a voice that almost broke Evelyn's heart.

"I'll have dinner later," she said, immediately regretting how it implied she'd be eating with her family while he was here, basically alone. "But I'll sit with you if you don't mind."

There was a long silence between them as he dished out his food, the clink of metal against the bowl the only sound. He sat at the table and picked up his spoon, but he didn't eat right away. Instead, his gaze drifted to the empty chair beside him, the space where Margaret should have been.

Evelyn waited, her heart tight in her chest before she finally spoke. "How... how are you holding up?" The words felt inadequate as soon as they left her mouth, but she said them anyway.

James let out a slow, pained breath, his gaze distant. "I'm not," he said, his voice barely above a whisper. "I should be, but I'm not. It's just—everything's so empty now," he murmured, his gaze far away. "Margaret, the baby... I can't seem to find my footing." He looked at her then, his eyes searching, as if he was hoping to find something to anchor him. "I wasn't ready. For none of it. I didn't know how to be a father, but I never got the chance."

His hands gripped the spoon tightly, the muscles in his jaw tightening. Evelyn's heart broke at the rawness in his voice, at the grief that had built up so quietly inside of him. She'd always seen him as steady, a man who carried the weight of his world without complaint. But this—this was different. This was the man beneath the surface, the man who had loved and lost, who was left with nothing but memories of what could have been.

"I'm sorry, James," she said softly, her words too small to fix anything, but she said them anyway. She didn't know what else to say, but something in her chest wouldn't let her look away from him—not this time.

He met her gaze then, his eyes wide and unguarded. "I never told her... I never told Margaret what she meant to me. Not enough. And now she's gone. She's gone, and I have nothing left but empty rooms and silence."

Evelyn's heart beat in her throat, the space between them suddenly fragile. He wasn't the man who fixed things. He wasn't the man who held the world together. He was a man like any other, lost and broken, searching for something to fill the void.

"You don't have to be alone, James," she said softly, the words slipping out before she could stop them.

She moved closer, instinctively, her hand reaching out across the table. His eyes flickered to her touch, but he didn't pull away. Instead, his hand found hers, the roughness of his palm brushing against her skin, and in that moment, everything seemed to shift. Her pulse quickened. She wasn't just here as a neighbor anymore. She was here as something more. Something that had been growing between them, unnamed, unspoken.

"I never wanted it to be like this," James whispered, his voice low, a rough edge to it.

She met his gaze. "I know." It wasn't just about Margaret and the baby anymore. It was about something deeper, something they had never let themselves acknowledge before.

He looked down at their hands, the tension thick in the air. The quiet stretched on, longer than it should have. His gaze met hers, and for a long moment, neither of them spoke. Then he slowly leaned forward, his hand tracing its way up her arm until he gently cupped her cheek. Evelyn's breath hitched, the world narrowing until there was only him, the warmth of his skin against hers, the weight of everything left unsaid between them.

And then, without another word, he kissed her. It was soft at first, hesitant, as if testing the waters of a feeling neither of them could quite name. Evelyn's eyes fluttered closed as her heart raced, her body pressing toward him almost instinctively. This was a moment both dangerous and inevitable, something that felt as if it had been waiting in the corners of her mind for far too long.

Evelyn stepped back, her breath shallow, her heart hammering in her chest. She blinked, her fingers trembling as she touched her lips, still tingling from the kiss. The world around her spun, as though the earth itself had shifted beneath her feet.

James stood a few paces away, his hands at his sides, his expression unreadable. His eyes, though, were full of something deep—something she couldn't name and didn't dare to try.

"I—" she started, but the words caught in her throat. What was there to say? How could she explain what had just happened? There was no going back now. The kiss had felt like a spark in a dry field, igniting everything in its path.

"I'm sorry," she whispered, barely audible, though the words were as much for herself as for him.

Even apart, she could still feel the warmth of his lips, and the thought alone was enough to send a shock of something deep through her, something that felt both like home and like a new beginning. A rush of emotion, raw and unfiltered, flowed between them, and Evelyn realized, with a quiet certainty, that she was no longer the same woman who had walked down that road just an hour ago.

She wiped her damp palms on her skirt, trying to regain some semblance of composure. Her chest tightened. Guilt bloomed in her stomach, sharp and bitter. What have we done? The thought stabbed her like a knife, but it didn't stop her feet from moving, urging her back toward the door, the way she had come.

James didn't speak. She couldn't bring herself to look back at him as she fled the room.

The door creaked shut behind her, and the cool air hit her face like a slap. She didn't pause; her feet were already moving, carrying her down the narrow, dust-swept road. Her breath came in ragged bursts as she ran, the gravel and dirt scratching her shoes, the sound of her heartbeat loud in her ears. It felt like she couldn't escape fast enough, but the farther she went, the heavier her guilt became. The shame. Why did I do that?

The farm came into view as she neared the bend in the road, but it didn't feel like home anymore. She wasn't sure where she was—or who she was—anymore. There was no one here to help her make sense of what had just happened.

The house loomed ahead, its familiar outline strangely foreign now. She couldn't see Thomas, couldn't hear Seth's laugh or the sound of the barn door creaking on its hinges. It was all too much, too sudden.

Evelyn pushed open the gate to the farm, her steps faltering. She took a deep, steadying breath, willing herself to look normal, to behave as though nothing had changed, as though nothing had shifted in her soul. But it had. And nothing would ever be the same.

She walked slowly toward the house, her mind racing, her body aching from the pressure of keeping her emotions locked tight. She had to act normal. She had to keep it together. Don't let Thomas see. The thought was her only anchor as she crossed the threshold into the house, her pulse still erratic.

Inside, the familiar scent of the morning's baked bread greeted her, but it offered no comfort. She closed the door behind her with a soft click, her breath shaky, her hands still trembling as she took off her coat. Every movement felt slow, as if the world around her had come to a standstill.

She had to keep going. She had to pretend.

And yet, as she stood there in the silence of the house, the weight of her own betrayal was unbearable. She hadn't just kissed James. She had crossed a line that could never be undone.

***

The days after the kiss were heavy with silence. Each time Evelyn saw James, it was as if the world had tilted just slightly, throwing everything into unfamiliar angles. The air felt thicker, more suffocating, though nothing had changed. And yet, everything had.

She had hoped the next time they crossed paths would feel normal, that she could pretend as if nothing had happened, but when she spotted him in the field one morning, his back turned as he tended to the hay bales, it was impossible to ignore the churn in her stomach.

Her feet faltered, the usual rhythm of her walk disrupted. She had always walked the path between their two farms without hesitation, but now, she found herself distracted by the small sound of her shoes on the dirt road, the rustle of wind in the tall grass. She glanced up as if by chance and saw James straighten up, dusting off his hands. His eyes caught hers, but there was no warmth in them—only a fleeting moment of acknowledgment before he looked away quickly, bending back down to his work.

The unease twisted in her chest. He's not looking at me like he used to, she thought, and the thought stung more than it should have.

She kept walking, not sparing another glance, but her hands felt clammy against the edge of her basket. The rest of the day dragged in an uncomfortable silence. Every time she crossed his path, it was the same. At the market, as she sorted through vegetables, her fingers brushed against the ripe tomatoes a little too harshly, trying not to meet his eyes. He lingered by the counter, pretending to look at the sacks of flour but never fully turning toward her.

When she finally glanced up, he was gone. It was a relief she hadn't expected. She wanted to call out to him, to break the barrier of quiet that had settled like dust between them, but the words never came. She found herself retreating back into her own thoughts, quietly wrapping her purchases, forcing her mind to settle.

Sunday came with its usual routine. The barn was full of hay and chatter as the families gathered at the small church. She could hear the buzz of conversation as she walked in after Thomas, holding hands with Seth, appreciating how her son's quiet presence offered her some comfort. She had hoped to disappear into the crowd, to make herself as small as possible, but as she stepped inside, she caught sight of him.

James was already seated in the back, his hat resting on the pew beside him, his gaze fixed on the altar but not really seeing it. Their eyes met for a heartbeat before she quickly turned her attention to the pulpit.

Just sit down, she told herself. Act normal.

Her hands tightened around the hymnal, the pages pressed hard between her fingers, and she kept her eyes forward. But there was something in the air that was too thick to ignore. The space between them felt too large, too small, too suffocating.

During the sermon, she found herself shifting in her seat, uncomfortable in the stillness. She avoided looking in his direction, but her mind kept drifting back to the moment they had shared. The feel of his lips on hers, the heat of his hand, the way it had felt so wrong and yet—so right. It gnawed at her, making it hard to sit still.

At the end of the service, she stood quickly, gathering Seth's hand in hers. She felt James' presence behind her, the weight of his gaze like a hand on her back. She could almost feel the words unsaid between them, an ache in her bones that neither of them dared to voice.

They both walked out of the church without speaking. Without a single word. The small-town air wrapped around her like a shroud. And though she was surrounded by the familiar faces of neighbors and friends, Evelyn felt more alone than ever.

Chapter Eleven

The Weight of Secrets

The chill of January clung to the morning air, turning every exhaled breath into a pale cloud. Evelyn adjusted her shawl tighter around her shoulders as she walked toward Willow Branch Road. She wasn't going anywhere in particular—just to the edge of the property where the fence posts leaned lazily against the wind—but every step carried an anticipation she didn't dare name.

She knew better. She told herself that each time. The weight of her life—her husband Thomas and little Seth, her mother's sharp voice, reminding her about propriety—all of it should have been enough to stop her feet. But it never did.

Rounding the bend where the road split toward James' property, Evelyn spotted a lone figure walking toward her, his silhouette framed by the rising sun. Her heart leaped before she could steady it. James.

He walked slower than usual, as though trying not to seem eager, but she could see the shift in his shoulders, the way his head turned just slightly, already knowing it was her before she spoke.

"Morning," she said, her voice calm, even. But her hands trembled as she clasped them in front of her.

"Morning, Evelyn," he replied. His voice was low, rough from the cold, but the warmth in it spread through her.

They stopped a few feet apart, both standing in the middle of the empty road. Around them, the world was quiet except for the faint rustle of branches in the wind.

"You're up early," he said, his mouth curving into a small smile. "Again."

"So are you."

James chuckled softly, looking down at the ground before meeting her gaze again. "Can't seem to help it."

Neither could she.

They lingered there, neither moving nor saying what they really wanted to say. His gloved hand twitched, and she wondered if he'd reach for her.

He didn't.

"I was just checking the fence," Evelyn lied, glancing toward the leaning posts.

"Fence looks fine to me," James replied, his eyes staying on her. The corners of his mouth twitched, not quite a smile, but enough to make her blush.

The tension between them was almost unbearable. Evelyn glanced up the road toward her house, then back to James.

"I shouldn't stay long," she said, though her feet didn't move.

"I know," he said, but he didn't move either.

Moments stretched into seconds that felt like hours. When she finally turned to go, her heart sank at the thought of leaving him. But she knew that in her house, not far away, her husband and son were waking and would be coming into the kitchen for breakfast, expecting to find her there. She had to keep her obligations.

***

Evelyn pressed her hand against the rough bark of the oak tree, the cool texture grounding her as she listened for any sign of movement. Her breath puffed in soft clouds in the crisp morning air, but her heart raced with the heat of anticipation. She had told herself not to come—again. Not to walk the narrow path to the edge of the forest, where the trees grew dense enough to shield them but still felt too exposed. Yet here she was as if drawn by an invisible tether.

The sound of a boot scuffing against fallen leaves made her turn. James stepped out from behind a cluster of young pines, his hat tilted low, shadowing his face. When he saw her, his mouth curved into that familiar smile—a little tentative, a little sad. Evelyn clutched her shawl tighter around her shoulders, though it did little to stop the warmth rushing through her.

"You came," he said, his voice low but steady.

Evelyn bit her lip, glancing back the way she'd come. She should leave, she knew it, but instead, she took a step closer. "I shouldn't have."

James nodded as though he understood, but his eyes lingered on her face, searching, softening. "I'm glad you did," he said.

Her resolve weakened further. The forest around them seemed to close in, muffling the rest of the world. She thought of the kiss they'd shared days ago, how it had left her both exhilarated and terrified. She'd replayed it a hundred times in her mind, trying to convince herself it was a mistake. But every time she closed her eyes, she felt his hand at her back, his breath against her cheek, the way he'd whispered her name like a promise.

Evelyn dropped her gaze to the ground. "James, we can't keep..."

"I know," he interrupted gently. "But here we are."

He stepped closer, and she caught his faint scent—fresh hay, a hint of tobacco. Her heart betrayed her again, skipping a beat. She hated how easily her defenses crumbled under his steady gaze, how much she longed to hear his voice, to feel his hand brush against hers, even for just a moment.

"Do you think about it?" he asked, his voice barely above a whisper. "That day in my kitchen?"

Evelyn's eyes snapped up to his. "I try not to," she admitted, though the words felt hollow. "It—it was wrong."

James exhaled slowly, tipping his hat back just enough for her to see the conflict etched across his face. "Maybe it was," he said, his tone gentle but firm. "But it didn't feel that way, not to me."

Her pulse quickened. "James," she began, but he reached out, taking her hand in his. His touch was warm, steady, and she felt herself leaning into it before she could think better of it.

"Just tell me one thing, Evelyn," he said, his thumb brushing lightly against her knuckles. "Do you regret it?"

The question hung between them, heavy with meaning. She could feel the weight of it pressing against her chest, but when she looked into his eyes, the truth slipped out before she could stop it.

"No," she whispered.

James's expression softened, his shoulders relaxing as though he'd been carrying the question himself. "Neither do I," he said.

For a moment, they simply stood there, the forest around them still and quiet, as if holding its breath. Evelyn felt the pull again, the undeniable force that had drawn her here, that made her heart ache even when she was alone.

"We have to be careful," she said finally, her voice trembling. "No one can know."

James nodded, his grip on her hand tightening slightly. "I know. We will."

He didn't let go, and neither did she. Instead, they stood there in the shadow of the trees, caught in a fragile moment that felt both impossible and inevitable. Evelyn knew the road ahead was dangerous, fraught with risks she couldn't yet see. But as James stepped closer, his presence steady and sure, she couldn't bring herself to pull away.

And for now... just for now, that was enough.

***

The lantern's soft glow flickered against the barn's weathered walls, casting long, wavering shadows over the stacks of hay and tools hung with deliberate care. Evelyn sat on a rough wooden bench, her hands folded tightly in her lap as if holding herself together. The night outside was still, except for the occasional rustle of leaves carried by the wind. She shouldn't be here, but she couldn't seem to stay away.

James sat opposite her, his posture relaxed but his gaze intent. His shirt sleeves were rolled to his elbows, and his hands rested loosely on his knees as though he were trying to appear casual despite the gravity in his eyes. Between them, the unspoken words hung heavier than the humid summer air.

"You don't have to stay long," James said softly, breaking the silence. His voice was gentle, careful, like he didn't want to spook her. "I just... I wanted to talk."

Evelyn's lips curved into a faint, humorless smile. "That's all we ever say, isn't it? Just to talk." Her gaze dropped to her hands. "But it feels like more than that."

James leaned forward, his elbows resting on his thighs. "What is it, then?" he asked. His voice carried no accusation, only quiet curiosity. "Because every time you leave, I tell myself it'll be the last. That I'll let you go. But then I see you again, Evelyn, and it feels like the first breath after drowning."

Her chest tightened. She looked up at him, startled by the genuineness of his words. "James..." She shook her head, trying to gather her thoughts. "This isn't... We can't—"

"I know," he interrupted, his tone firm but not unkind. "I know it isn't right. But that doesn't make it any less real."

She swallowed hard. "Thomas is a good man," she said, her voice trembling. "He works hard, he's loyal. He... he doesn't deserve this."

James tilted his head, his expression softening. "And you?" he asked. "What do you deserve?"

The question cut through her like a knife. No one had ever asked her that before. Not her parents, not Thomas, not even herself. She stared at James, searching his face for some kind of answer, but all she found was a reflection of her own longing.

"I don't know," she admitted, her voice barely above a whisper.

He reached out then, his calloused hand covering hers. The touch was warm, steady, grounding. Evelyn didn't pull away. Instead, she let herself feel it—the connection, the comfort, the terrifying depth of it all.

"You deserve to be seen," James said, his thumb brushing lightly over her knuckles. "To be heard. To have someone who knows every part of you, even the parts you're afraid to show."

A lump rose in her throat. "Thomas tries," she said, though the words felt hollow. "He just... he doesn't understand me. Not the way you do."

James's gaze didn't waver. "And how is that?" he asked quietly.

Evelyn hesitated, the weight of her emotions threatening to spill over. "You make me feel like... like I'm not just a wife or a mother or someone doing what's expected. With you, I can say what I'm thinking, what I'm feeling, and you—" Her voice broke. "You listen. You don't judge me. You don't... dismiss me."

He nodded slowly, his eyes never leaving hers. "Because I see you, Evelyn. All of you. And I think about you—every day, every night. Even when I shouldn't."

The confession hung in the air, raw and unvarnished. Evelyn's breath hitched, and for a moment, she thought about running, about leaving before the pull between them became too strong to resist. But then James's hand tightened around hers, anchoring her in place.

Evelyn opened her mouth, the words trembling on the edge of her lips. But instead of telling him how she felt, she leaned forward, her forehead resting against his.

In the quiet sanctuary of the barn, surrounded by shadows and secrets, they let themselves fall deeper into a love they couldn't name, a love they couldn't claim. It was dangerous, impossible, but in that moment, it was everything.

***

The ticking of the clock on the mantle seemed louder than usual, filling the quiet of the parlor like a metronome for Evelyn's thoughts. She sat in her favorite armchair, a basket of mending at her feet, but her hands remained idle in her lap. The needle and thread she'd picked up earlier had fallen unnoticed, her mind elsewhere.

Thomas sat across the room, the day's newspaper open in his hands, the crisp rustle of pages punctuating the silence. The familiar sight of her husband, comfortable and steady, should have brought her peace. Instead, it stirred an ache she couldn't name, a restless unease that had taken root deep in her chest.

"Dinner was good tonight," Thomas said without looking up. "You always know just how to make the stew taste right."

Evelyn forced a small smile, though he wasn't watching to see it. "Thank you," she replied softly. Her voice sounded foreign to her, as if it came from someone else.

The praise should have warmed her. Once, it would have. But now, it only highlighted the chasm that had opened between them—a chasm filled with things left unsaid. She stared at the floor, tracing the grain of the wood with her eyes, as if the pattern might offer answers to questions she couldn't bring herself to ask.

Thomas turned another page, oblivious to her turmoil. He was a good man, steady and hardworking, just as her parents had promised when they arranged their match. He cared for her, provided for her, never raised his voice or his hand. But his kindness only deepened her guilt. How could she think of James while sitting here, on the land Thomas worked hard to keep running for her?

Her breath caught at the thought of James. She could see him so clearly—his weathered hands, the way his eyes softened when he looked at her, the way he listened like every word she said mattered. That feeling, so intoxicating, had become her undoing.

She pressed her palms into her lap, her nails pressing into her skin. This has to stop, she told herself. You're a wife. A mother. You made a promise. But even as she tried to summon resolve, her mind betrayed her, drifting back to the edge of the woods where James had waited for her just yesterday. His words, his touch, his presence—it all lingered, impossible to forget.

"Everything all right?" Thomas's voice broke through her reverie. She looked up sharply, meeting his gaze. His brow was furrowed in mild concern; the paper lowered in his lap.

"Yes," she said quickly, too quickly. "Just tired."

He nodded, satisfied with her answer, and returned to his reading. The moment passed, but Evelyn's pulse continued to race. She rose from her chair, needing an escape, some excuse to leave the room.

"I'll make some tea," she murmured, though she doubted he heard her.

In the kitchen, Evelyn leaned against the counter, gripping its edge as if it might anchor her. The room felt stifling, though the windows were open, and the night air carried the faint scent of honeysuckle. Her reflection in the windowpane startled her. She looked pale, her eyes wide and shadowed. A stranger stared back.

"Get hold of yourself," she whispered. But how could she? Every part of her life felt like it was splitting in two—the life she was meant to lead and the one her heart seemed to crave.

She busied herself boiling water and steeping tea leaves, the motions mechanical. When she returned to the parlor, cup in hand, Thomas hadn't moved. He glanced up briefly, giving her the faintest of smiles, before turning back to the paper. The interaction was simple, unremarkable, the kind that made up most of their days. Yet it felt unbearably heavy, laden with everything she was hiding.

As she sipped the tea, its heat spreading through her chest, Evelyn knew she couldn't keep this up forever. The weight of her guilt pressed down on her, growing heavier with each passing day. But what could she do? There was no way to undo what had already begun, no way to silence her heart without tearing herself apart.

She glanced at Thomas, his face serene in the glow of the lamp. He didn't deserve this betrayal. But James's face lingered in her mind, his voice echoing in her memory. How could she choose between the life she'd built and the love she'd found?

The clock chimed, its sound sharp and jarring. Evelyn flinched, the spell of her thoughts broken. She set her cup down and folded her hands in her lap once more, resolved to keep her secret for one more night. For one more day. But deep down, she knew the truth: her heart was no longer hers to give.

***

Willow Branch Road was quiet except for the occasional bird chirping along the way. Evelyn stood near the oak tree, her fingers fidgeting with the hem of her apron. She stared out into the twilight, where the sun sank low, bathing the fields in hues of gold and crimson. The horizon blurred as her mind raced.

Behind her, a crunch in the leaves made her pulse jump. She turned sharply, and there he was—James. He didn't speak; he just tipped his hat slightly before taking it off, holding it in his hands.

"I wasn't sure you'd come," Evelyn said, her voice softer than she intended.

"I wasn't sure I should," he admitted, his voice low, rough like the gravel road that separated their lives. "But here I am."

They stood in silence for a moment, the distance between them feeling both unbearable and necessary. James took a step closer, his boots kicking up pebbles from the road. Evelyn didn't move, though every instinct screamed for her to either close the space between them or run from it.

"This can't go on, James," she said finally, her words trembling. "It's only a matter of time before someone notices."

"I know," he said, stopping a few feet away from her. He tilted his head slightly, studying her face as though memorizing it. "But I can't stop. Can you?"

Evelyn pressed her lips together, the truth rising bitter and unspoken in her throat. "We're being selfish," she whispered. "This isn't just about us. If Thomas—"

"Thomas is a good man," James interrupted gently, his eyes shadowed with something like shame. "I'm not saying he isn't. But does that mean you have to give up everything you feel? Everything we've—"

"Don't," she said sharply, cutting him off. Her voice broke, and she turned away, bracing herself against the tree trunk. "Don't make this harder than it already is."

James hesitated, then stepped closer. His hand hovered just over her shoulder, as though afraid to touch her. "Evelyn," he murmured, "we can figure this out. Maybe there's a way—"

"And do what?" She spun around, her eyes wet and furious. "Run off together? Leave Seth, leave Thomas? Ruin two families? What kind of life would that be?"

His jaw clenched, and he looked down at his hat, twisting it between his hands. "I don't have the answers," he said after a long pause. "I wish I did. But what I know is, I can't keep pretending I don't love you."

Evelyn felt the words hit her like a physical blow. Her chest tightened, and for a moment, she let herself imagine a world where it wasn't wrong, where loving James didn't mean breaking everything else.

But that world didn't exist.

"We're going to get caught," she said, her voice almost a plea. "And when we do, there won't be any fixing this. There'll only be wreckage."

James stepped closer again, closing the distance this time. He reached for her, his hands settling on her arms. She didn't pull away. "Then tell me to walk away," he said, his voice low and steady. "Right now, tell me to leave, and I swear I'll go. But if you can't—"

"I can't," she admitted, her voice barely a whisper.

They stood like that for what felt like an eternity, the weight of their choices pressing down on them. Evelyn leaned her forehead against his chest, feeling the steady rhythm of his heartbeat beneath her cheek. They stayed huddled together, two people caught in a storm of their own making, unsure of where to go next.

Chapter Twelve

Dear James

April 12, 1933

Dear James,

I find myself stealing moments in the quiet of the evening to write to you. The house is still, save for the rhythmic creak of the rocking chair in the parlor, where Thomas has drifted off with the day's paper resting on his chest. It is in these moments of calm, when the world feels far away, that my thoughts turn to you. I shouldn't be putting any of this to paper—I know that as well as you—but the words seem to pour out as though they've been waiting for me to give them shape.

I can't help but think of this afternoon, the way the sunlight danced through the trees while we walked along the creek. It felt like the world had carved out that small sliver of time just for us. Brief as it was, I carry it with me now, a flicker of warmth against the shadows that creep in when you're not near.

The little wooden bird you carved has found a place on the windowsill in the kitchen, where it catches the morning light. Seth asked me about it yesterday. He said it looked like the ones that flit around the dogwood tree by the barn. I told him it was a gift, but not from whom. He didn't press further—children seldom see beyond what they're told—but I found myself smiling at the thought of you whittling away at a scrap of wood, your hands as steady as ever.

The flower, too, rests nearby, tucked into the drawer of my sewing table. It reminds me of the time you caught me humming in the garden, and I wondered if you knew how much those simple moments meant to me. And the box—it is perhaps my favorite. I've placed the tiniest treasures inside, things no one else would think twice about but that I can't bear to lose. Each piece you've made feels like a small part of you, and I keep them close to remind me that this is real, even when it feels like a dream I shouldn't be having.

James, I must confess, there are days I wish things were different. That we didn't have to steal away like shadows, always glancing over our shoulders. I wish I could sit beside you on your porch without feeling the weight of the world pressing down or walk into town with you without a thousand questions hanging in the air.

But these are just wishes, and wishing won't change the life we've built or the one I've promised to uphold. Still, your presence has brought a light into my days that I didn't know I was missing. You make me laugh in a way I haven't in years, and for that, I am endlessly grateful.

I know what we're doing is dangerous and wrong. I think about it every time I see you, and yet, I keep coming back. I tell myself it's just for today, just one more moment, and then I'll let you go. But as I write these words, I know in my heart that I can't imagine my days without you in them now.

I don't know how long this will last or how it will end, but for now, I hold tightly to what we have. If the world ever takes this from us, I want you to know how much you mean to me, how much you've changed my days and my heart.

Until I see you again,
Evelyn

Chapter Thirteen

The Deep Connection

The cicadas buzzed in the heavy summer air, their drone stretching across the quiet fields like a hymn. Evelyn stood on the porch, her hand resting lightly on the weathered railing. The sun had slipped low in the sky, bathing the farm in shades of amber and gold. It should have been a beautiful evening, the kind that invited soft words and shared silences, but Evelyn felt the weight of the day pressing on her chest.

Thomas was in the barn fixing something—or at least pretending to. The truth was, he spent more time tinkering with tools than he did sitting beside her these days. She stepped off the porch, her shoes crunching on the dirt path as she made her way toward him.

The barn door creaked as she pushed it open, revealing Thomas hunched over a workbench. His sleeves were rolled up, revealing tanned, muscular arms flecked with sawdust. He didn't look up.

"Thomas," she said, her voice tentative but steady.

"Hm?" He grabbed a wrench and twisted it against the bolts of a rusted plow, the sound grating in the otherwise still barn.

"Do you think we could sit out on the porch tonight? Just the two of us?"

He paused, finally glancing up. His face was lined with exhaustion, but there was something else there, too—a distance she didn't know how to bridge.

"Maybe," he said, wiping his hands on a rag. "Got a lot to finish here, though. Can't afford to let things slip."

Evelyn bit the inside of her cheek, the taste of iron sharp on her tongue. "It's just... it's been a while since we've talked, really talked. I miss you."

Thomas blinked as if the words confused him. He scratched his jaw, where a day's worth of stubble shadowed his face. "I'm here, ain't I?"

She nodded slowly, folding her arms. "You're here, but not really here, Thomas. It feels like the farm gets more of you than I do."

He frowned, his lips pressing into a thin line. "You think this farm runs itself? I'm doing this for us, Evelyn. For Seth. So he's got something to inherit one day."

"I know that," she said softly. "But what about now? What about us?"

Thomas sighed, turning back to the plow. "This ain't the time for this kind of talk. I've got work to do."

The finality in his tone stung, but Evelyn wasn't ready to give up. She stepped closer, her hand brushing his arm. "Thomas, please. I just need—"

"I said, not now," he snapped, his voice louder than he intended. He glanced at her, guilt flashing across his face before he turned back to the workbench. "We'll talk later, alright?"

But Evelyn knew they wouldn't. She stood there for a moment, the silence between them thick and heavy, before stepping back. Her hand fell to her side.

"Alright," she murmured, though the word tasted bitter. She turned and walked out of the barn, the warm evening air doing little to soothe her frayed nerves.

As she made her way back toward the house, Evelyn's eyes strayed to the horizon, where Willow Branch Road snaked its way through the fields and into the woods. James's farm was just beyond those trees. She imagined him sitting on his porch, his pipe in hand, gazing out at the same sunset she could see.

With James, the silences were different. They weren't walls but invitations—spaces for her to fill with her thoughts, her dreams, her frustrations. He listened when she spoke, his dark eyes warm and attentive, as though every word she said mattered.

She shook her head as if the motion could dislodge the thoughts that had begun to creep in more often than they should. She loved Thomas. She had married him and shared a life with him. But as the years had worn on, she couldn't ignore the growing void between them—a void that James now seemed to fill so effortlessly.

Evelyn reached the porch and sank into the rocking chair, staring out at the fields that stretched endlessly before her. The farm was Thomas's world, and she had once thought it would be hers, too. But she wanted more. And now, as the shadows lengthened and the cicadas sang their mournful song, she couldn't shake the feeling that she was as invisible to him as the breeze rustling through the corn.

***

The aroma of rosemary and roasted chicken filled the kitchen, mingling with the buttery scent of freshly baked bread. Evelyn wiped her hands on her apron and stepped back to admire the small feast she had managed to assemble despite the day's relentless chores. The good china was set on the table—a rare indulgence—and a vase of early summer wildflowers she had gathered from the field that morning sat in the center. She felt like this was the perfect way to try and rekindle the spark with Thomas.

She glanced at the clock. He would be in soon; the sun had started its slow descent, gilding the tops of the trees outside the window. She had already put Seth to bed and the sweet boy had gone willingly, tired out from a long afternoon of play after school. It would be just the adults tonight, and she hoped it would feel like they were courting again. She smoothed the skirt of her best dress, a soft blue one with a fitted waist that had once made Thomas whistle when they were newlyweds. The memory flickered faintly, a distant warmth she couldn't quite hold onto.

The sound of the screen door creaking open snapped her to attention. Thomas entered, his boots heavy on the floor, his shirt stained with sweat and dust from the field. He paused in the doorway, his broad frame nearly filling it, his eyes flicking to the table before settling on her.

"What's all this?" he asked, his voice neutral.

"I thought we could have a nice dinner," Evelyn said, folding her hands in front of her. "It's been a while since we sat down together like this."

Thomas nodded but didn't respond. He moved to the sink, rolling up his sleeves to wash his hands. The water splashed loudly against the basin as Evelyn stood in the center of the room, her heart sinking under the weight of his silence.

"Smells good," he offered after a moment, drying his hands on a dishtowel.

"Thank you," she said, forcing a smile. She gestured toward the table. "Come, sit. I'll pour us some sweet tea."

Thomas obliged, pulling out a chair and lowering himself into it with a weary grunt. Evelyn busied herself with the tea, her hands trembling slightly as she poured.

"How was your day?" she asked, setting the glasses down and taking her seat across from him.

"Busy," he replied, spearing a piece of chicken with his fork. "The south field's gonna need replanting. That storm last week drowned half the crop."

Evelyn nodded, though she had already known as much. She had seen him out there, knee-deep in mud, cursing under his breath as he surveyed the damage.

"I could help," she offered tentatively.

Thomas shook his head. "You've got enough to do around here."

For a while, the only sounds were the clink of silverware against plates and the steady hum of crickets outside the open window. Evelyn stole glances at him, searching for the man she used to know—the one who had once leaned close to whisper jokes in her ear, who had taken her hand in the barn and kissed her until she laughed.

She tried again. "Do you remember the time we took a picnic down by the lake? It was spring, and you caught that big catfish with your bare hands." She smiled, hoping the memory would coax a similar one from him.

Thomas glanced up briefly, his brow furrowing as though he were trying to recall it. "Yeah," he said after a moment, but his tone was flat, and he didn't elaborate.

Evelyn's chest tightened. She reached across the table, her hand brushing his. "Thomas, do you think—"

"Do you mind passing the butter?" he interrupted, pulling his hand away.

Her fingers curled into a fist, retreating to her lap. She swallowed the lump rising in her throat and passed the dish.

As the meal wore on, Evelyn felt her resolve slipping. She had tried, hadn't she? The nice meal, the dress, the effort to draw him out. But Thomas seemed as unreachable as ever, his thoughts tethered to the farm, his words brief and practical.

When he pushed back his chair and thanked her for dinner, his tone polite but distant, Evelyn watched him go with a mix of sadness and resignation. The screen door creaked again as he stepped onto the porch, and soon, she heard the scrape of his chair as he settled into his usual spot, gazing out at the darkening fields.

Evelyn stood in the kitchen, staring at the empty plates on the table. She began clearing the dishes, glad to have the mindless chore to distract her from her thoughts and feelings.

Later, as she lay in bed, staring at the ceiling, she couldn't stop herself from thinking about James—about the way his eyes lit up when he saw her, the way he listened as though her words were worth something. She tried to shove the thoughts away, but they came unbidden, warm, and inviting, a contrast to the cold distance that had settled between her and Thomas.

Evelyn turned onto her side, clutching the quilt to her chest. She had tried. But as the moonlight spilled through the window, casting long shadows across the room, she couldn't help but wonder if it was enough—or if it ever could be.

***

Despite last week's special dinner not turning out the way she intended, Evelyn was determined to try again. Thinking maybe Thomas was just oblivious, too focused on the farm, she flat-out told him what she was doing that morning.

"I thought dinner together tonight might be nice," she said.

"We eat dinner together every night," Thomas said in his typical straightforward manner.

"Right, but tonight will be without Seth. So we can talk." She shot him a meaningful look, but it seemed to go right over his head.

"Well then, I guess I better be prepared," he said, slapping his hands on his thighs as he got up to start his day.

Evelyn felt a warm flutter in her belly. See, this was what it could be like if they both tried! If he knew it was coming, he would make an effort.

"What are we going to talk about?" he asked, catching her off guard.

"What do you mean?"

"Is there something on your mind?" He looked at her like his line of thinking was obvious, and as soon as he spoke the words, it slapped Evelyn across the face.

Of course he wants to talk about something. He won't just let his thoughts roam and share what passes through his head, like James and I do... No, she couldn't think that way, not with her husband standing right in front of her.

She cleared her throat as if that could also clear her mind. "Just talk about whatever's on our minds. Hopes, dreams, all that jazz."

Thomas made a face. "I don't think I've got much on my mind other than the farm," he said.

Evelyn scrunched her nose at him behind his back. Like that statement was a surprise to anyone!

"Speaking of, I better get to it," he said, walking toward the back door to put on his boots and get to work.

"See you tonight," Evelyn said, determined to make her plan happen no matter how stubborn her husband was.

Hours later, the kitchen glowed with the soft light of the kerosene lamp, its golden halo catching the edges of the polished silverware and the neatly folded linen napkins Evelyn had carefully arranged. The roast sat in the center of the table, a proud crown of browned perfection surrounded by roasted vegetables she had pulled from their garden. She smoothed her apron, glancing once more at the place settings. Everything was just so.

From the open doorway, she could hear Seth's faint giggles as he played with the tin soldiers Thomas had carved for him last Christmas. Evelyn had coaxed him to room earlier than usual once more, promising he could stay up late tomorrow if only he gave her this one evening. He'd gone without much fuss, always her sweet boy, though his independence felt like a blade cutting both ways. He no longer needed her the way he once had, and Thomas—well, Thomas never seemed to need her at all.

The thought bit at her as she peeked out the kitchen window. The barn door stood ajar, faint lamplight spilling onto the dirt path. She waited, listening for the heavy tread of her husband's boots on the porch.

It didn't come.

She watched the sky get darker, wondering if she should go out and tell him dinner was ready. But he knew. He knew their routines, and besides, he had to be getting hungry by now. She wasn't going to nag or mother him. He could come in when he was ready.

She settled into a chair at the table, glancing between the place settings and the oven, where she wondered if she should keep the food warm.

As the sky beyond the kitchen window turned completely black, Evelyn sighed and stood up. The food was certainly cold by now, and reheating it would make it tough, but it had to be done. She carried the roast back to the oven, put it back in the skillet, and slid it into the oven. She was scooping the vegetables back into their pot when the door finally opened. Her heart skipped, anticipation warring with dread.

"There you are," she said, masking her anger with a smile. "I've just started warming up our supper."

Thomas grunted, far from an apology, and hung his hat on the hook near the door. His boots left faint tracks across the freshly scrubbed floor, but Evelyn swallowed her irritation. He washed his hands at the basin without a word, the water splashing heavily as he scrubbed away the grime of the day.

"Seth is playing in his room," she offered, her voice light, hopeful. "So we can take our time and talk about whatever's on our minds."

He nodded absently, drying his hands on a towel. "Good. Got a long day tomorrow. Need a solid meal."

Evelyn's chest tightened, her carefully planned words faltering. She busied herself pouring water into his glass, but the silence between them felt heavier than the iron skillet she'd used for the roast. She got everything back out of the oven and placed it on the table. It didn't look as nice as it had when she sat there alone. Everything looked sad, limp, and dingy.

Thomas sat, his chair scraping against the floor, and began serving himself without a glance in her direction. Evelyn followed, sitting across from him, her hands folded neatly in her lap.

"Well," she said after a moment, "how are the fields looking? Did the rain help?"

"Some," he replied with a mouthful of food. "Still need to fix the south fence. Cows'll wander if it isn't done by the weekend."

She nodded, biting the inside of her cheek. He didn't comment on the roast, the vegetables, or the fact that she'd lit a small candle in the center of the table—something she hadn't done since Seth was born. She couldn't even tell if he noticed since it was practically burned down to nothing now.

As the meal dragged on, Evelyn's smile grew tighter, her replies more clipped. She asked about the livestock, the tools, anything to draw him into conversation, but his answers remained short, distracted. He thanked her for dinner when he'd finished, standing to rinse his plate without meeting her eyes.

Evelyn remained at the table, staring at her untouched plate long after Thomas had retreated upstairs, claiming he was too tired to even read the paper. She tried to tell herself that tiredness was why he hadn't wanted to have a conversation tonight, but she couldn't ignore the lump forming in her throat.

Her eyes burned as she thought of how carefully she had planned the evening, how she'd ironed her dress and braided her hair the way he used to like it when they were courting. She had wanted him to see her, not just as the woman who kept the house running and fed his son, but as the girl he had once asked to dance on the church lawn.

But Thomas didn't see her. Not anymore. Perhaps he never truly had. He couldn't even be bothered to come inside at dinnertime, even though he knew she'd planned a special evening. Or was it because he'd known she'd planned a special evening? Maybe he simply didn't want to be around her anymore.

The loneliness pressed against her chest, heavy and unrelenting. She glanced toward the window, the distant silhouette of the trees on the horizon. Somewhere beyond them was James, who made her feel like someone worth noticing.

She shouldn't be thinking of him, not like this. But no matter how hard she tried, she couldn't push the thought away.

Evelyn stood abruptly, gathering the dishes and scrubbing them with a ferocity that left her arms aching. When the last plate was dried, and the candle snuffed out, she climbed the stairs in silence.

As she lay in bed, staring at the cracks in the ceiling, she made herself admit what she had been denying for too long: Thomas would never be the man she needed him to be. And now, with that realization sitting heavy in her chest, the image of James felt closer, brighter—a dangerous spark in the darkness of her quiet, unfulfilled life.

Chapter Fourteen

The Two Lives

The summer heat lingered, though September's cooler whispers had begun to weave through the air. Evelyn stood at the kitchen counter, hands deep in a basin of scalding water, scrubbing the remnants of tomato skins from the day's canning. Steam curled up from the pot on the stove, its hiss punctuating the heavy silence of the house. The pantry shelves behind her gleamed with jars of peaches, green beans, and pickled cucumbers, each sealed with the care of a woman who knew the long winter ahead depended on her efforts.

Through the open window above the sink, Seth's faint laughter reached her ears. He was chasing the barn cat again, his little boots thudding against the dirt yard. Evelyn smiled faintly, but the expression didn't reach her eyes. She dipped another jar into the hot water, the cloth in her hand moving in circles, over and over.

Thomas had been in the fields since dawn, his routine as steady and predictable as the sunrise. There had been no words between them this morning except for his gruff request for coffee and the sharp creak of his chair as he left the table. Evelyn didn't expect more. She had long since learned that expecting anything else only led to disappointment.

The jar slipped from her hands, and she cursed softly, fumbling to catch it before it shattered. It landed back in the basin with a splash, soaking her apron and the front of her dress. Evelyn sighed, pulling the apron off and draping it over a chair. She leaned against the counter, staring out the window.

The willow trees lining Willow Branch Road swayed in the breeze, their drooping branches hiding the narrow path that led to James's farm. Her gaze lingered there longer than she meant it to, her chest tightening with the ache she carried daily.

Though she had been determined to stay away, she had gone to his farm the week before, bringing over a jar of blackberry preserves as an excuse. James had been out by the fence line, mending a post, his sleeves rolled up and his hair damp with sweat. They had spoken in quiet tones, their words simple and practical, but his eyes had lingered on her in a way that made her heart quicken.

The memory burned, and Evelyn forced herself to turn away from the window. She couldn't keep thinking about him—not when there was so much to do. The garden still needed weeding, and there were bushels of apples to sort in the barn.

Her hands found the rhythm of work again, but her mind was elsewhere. She loved Seth fiercely, and her pride in her home was real, but there was a part of her—a part she didn't even recognize anymore—that felt trapped. Trapped in the endless cycle of duty and silence. Trapped in a house where her voice was another sound to be tuned out.

The back door creaked, and Seth burst in, cheeks flushed and grinning. He held up a crooked stick, declaring it his sword. Evelyn turned to him, her smile softer this time, her fingers brushing the damp curls from his forehead.

"Be sure to leave the chickens alone with that sword of yours," she said, her tone light despite the heaviness inside her.

"I'm not scared of chickens, Mama," Seth replied, puffing his chest out.

"You're not scared of much," she said, the corners of her mouth twitching upward. "Now go wash up. Supper will be ready soon."

Seth darted off, his laughter trailing behind him. Evelyn watched him go, her heart swelling with love and breaking all at once.

The pot on the stove boiled over, and she moved to lower the heat, wiping her hands on her dress. The days were always full, but it wasn't the kind of fullness that satisfied her. It was the kind that left her hollow, as if she were pouring herself into this house, this family, and leaving nothing left for her own heart.

She stirred the pot absently, the scent of tomatoes filling the kitchen. Outside, the willow branches danced in the breeze, and beyond them, James's house waited, as steady and quiet as her longing.

Evelyn pressed her palm to her chest, as though she could quiet the ache that had settled there. She knew she would finish the supper, tend to Seth, and wait for Thomas to come in without a word of thanks. She would clean the dishes, fold the laundry, and keep up appearances, all while the other life—the one she wasn't supposed to want—breathed quietly beneath the surface.

For now, she would stay in this one. But she wasn't sure how much longer she could.

***

The sun was setting low over the fields, bathing the horizon in gold and deep violet. Evelyn's hands rested on the wooden gate that divided her land from James's, its rough surface pressing against her palms. She glanced back toward the house, where the faint glow of a lantern in the kitchen window signaled Thomas and Seth were settled for the evening. Her heart thudded in her chest as she turned toward the path that wound through the grove of trees and led to James's barn.

He was there, as he'd promised. The door was cracked open, and the soft hum of his voice carried on the breeze. He was talking to one of the horses, murmuring something soothing as he brushed its flank. She stepped inside, the earthy scent of hay and animals wrapping around her like a familiar embrace.

James turned at the sound of her footsteps, his face breaking into a slow, easy smile. "Evenin', Evelyn," he said, his voice warm and calm, like a river at twilight.

"Good evening, James," she replied, the words coming out softer than she intended. She folded her hands in front of her, feeling suddenly shy beneath his gaze.

"Long day?" he asked, setting the brush down and stepping toward her.

"Aren't they all?" She laughed lightly, but there was an edge to it. "The canning's done, the garden's weeded, and supper's put away. That should be enough, but somehow, it never feels like it is."

James nodded, leaning against a nearby stall. "You do enough for ten people, Evelyn. Don't let anyone make you feel otherwise."

She looked at him then, and the sincerity in his eyes nearly undid her. There was no pretense with James, no need to hold herself in check. He saw her—really saw her—and that was something she hadn't felt in years.

"Sometimes, I wonder if I even know who I am anymore," she said quietly, her gaze falling to the barn floor. "Everything I do is for the house, the family, the farm. I don't mind it—not really. But there are moments..." Her voice trailed off, and she shook her head.

James stepped closer, his boots crunching against the hay-strewn ground. "Moments where you feel like you're not in there at all," he said, gesturing toward her house with a tilt of his head.

Her breath caught, and she nodded. "Yes."

They stood in silence for a moment, the weight of unspoken truths filling the space between them. Finally, James broke it. "I reckon that's why you came tonight. To remember who you are."

Evelyn looked up at him, her heart pounding. "And who am I, James?"

His eyes softened, and he gave her that crooked smile that always made her chest ache. "You're the woman who sings to herself when she's picking apples. The one who knows every name and use for the herbs in her garden. The woman who lights up when she talks about books and stories." He paused, his voice growing quieter. "And the one who deserves to feel seen. To feel... free."

Her throat tightened, and for a moment, she couldn't speak. She wanted to tell him how much those words meant, how much he meant. Instead, she reached out, her fingers brushing against his.

"Thank you," she whispered.

James took her hand in his, his touch steady and sure. "You don't have to thank me, Evelyn. Just don't forget who you are. Don't let yourself disappear."

She felt tears prick her eyes, but she blinked them away, letting herself smile instead. "I don't feel invisible when I'm with you," she admitted, her voice barely above a whisper.

He squeezed her hand gently. "Then stay a little longer. You deserve to feel like yourself again."

She let the warmth of his presence seep into the parts of her that had grown cold and distant. For the first time in weeks—maybe months—Evelyn felt like she could breathe.

But she knew she couldn't stay. She didn't want Thomas looking for her... if he even noticed she wasn't around.

"I'll come back," she promised James as she turned to leave.

The sensation of his hand on hers was enough to help her get through the night. Thomas didn't realize Evelyn had been gone and would never suspect she was sneaking over to see the neighbor. He was too fixated on the farm and his own narrow vision to see what his wife was going through.

But it didn't bother Evelyn that night as she watched Thomas go into Seth's bedroom to sleep and she turned and went into her own. She knew James saw her. He knew her heart, and that was enough to satisfy her for now.

***

After several days of rain, Evelyn was feeling stir-crazy. She'd baked biscuits and tried to stretch the sugar to make a cake. She'd cleaned the house from top to bottom. She'd kept busy, trying to work off her nervous energy, but what she really needed help controlling were her thoughts.

They centered on James.

And finally, the storm had passed, though it left the air heavy with the scent of rain-soaked earth. But the break in the clouds was enough for Evelyn to slip on her boots and pull a jacket over her head, just in case, and make a break for James's house while Thomas and Seth worked together in the fields, checking for flooding.

She slipped into James's barn and saw him leaning against the workbench as if he'd been waiting for her. His sleeves were rolled up, and a faint sheen of sweat glistened on his forearms. His shirt clung to him, damp from repairing the roof after the downpour. Evelyn's eyes traced the sharp lines of his jaw, the way his hair curled at the ends, still wet. His presence filled the space and made her feel safe yet out of control at the same time.

"You didn't have to bring these," he said finally, his voice low and rough. He held the tin of biscuits in his hand as though it were precious, his thumb brushing over the lid.

"I know," she said, her voice barely above a whisper. "I wanted to."

Silence fell between them, broken only by the soft rustle of the horses in their stalls. Evelyn's heart beat painfully in her chest, loud enough that she was sure James could hear it. The weight of all the unspoken moments between them seemed to press down like the heavy air after the rain.

"I've been thinking about you," James said, so softly she almost didn't hear it.

Her breath caught, and she looked up at him. His eyes met hers then, and there was no mistaking the longing there, the need that mirrored her own.

"James," she started, her voice trembling. She wanted to admit that she was thinking about him, too, but suddenly, all her nerve was gone, and she just felt uncertain. "This isn't—"

"Don't," he interrupted, stepping closer. "Don't say it's not right or that we shouldn't. I know all of that, Evelyn. I know it better than anyone. But every time you walk away, I feel like I'm losing something I never should've had to begin with."

The confession hit her like a wave, and her resolve cracked under its weight. Tears stung her eyes, and she shook her head, trying to find the words to push him away, to make him understand. But then his hand was on her cheek, warm and calloused, and the world seemed to fall away.

"I can't keep pretending," he said, his voice breaking. "Not with you standing here. Not when you look at me like that."

Her lips parted to protest, to say something, but before she could, his mouth was on hers. The kiss was desperate, full of everything they'd held back for too long. She gasped against him, her hands gripping his shirt as though to steady herself, and he pulled her closer, his arms wrapping around her like he could shield her from the storm they were creating.

The hay beneath their feet muffled their movements as they stumbled back, his hand finding the small of her back, hers tangling in his hair. The scent of him—soap and sweat and rain—filled her senses, drowning out the guilt that clawed at the edges of her mind.

"Evelyn," he murmured against her lips, her name a prayer and a plea all at once.

She pulled back just enough to look at him, her fingers tracing the line of his jaw. His eyes searched hers, filled with both tenderness and torment.

"This will change everything," she whispered, the truth of it hanging between them like the storm clouds that had only just cleared.

"I know," he said, his voice steady. "But it doesn't change how I feel about you."

For a moment, she thought about running, about leaving the barn and never looking back. But the thought of a life without him, without this, was more unbearable than the shame she knew would follow.

With trembling hands, she reached up and pulled him back to her, the last of her resistance crumbling. The kiss deepened, and the world outside the barn disappeared, leaving only the two of them and the forbidden fire they couldn't extinguish.

Somewhere in the back of her mind, Evelyn knew there would be consequences. But for now, in James's arms, she allowed herself to forget.

***

The morning sunlight filtered through the lace curtains in Evelyn's kitchen, painting the worn wooden table with patches of gold. The aroma of freshly brewed coffee filled the air, but Evelyn barely noticed. She stood at the sink, hands submerged in soapy water, scrubbing a plate that had been clean for several minutes. Her movements were mechanical, her mind elsewhere—back in James's barn, where she'd left a part of herself the night before.

She shut her eyes tightly, willing the memories away, but they surged forward like a flood breaking through a dam. The way his hand had lingered on hers, rough but tender. The way his lips had searched hers with a desperation she recognized in herself. The way they'd clung to each other as if the world outside didn't exist.

Her stomach churned.

Behind her, the creak of the floorboards signaled Thomas's approach. Evelyn straightened, gripping the edge of the sink. His steps were slow and heavy, and she could feel his presence before he even spoke.

"Coffee smells good," he said, his voice gruff but warm.

She turned to him with a practiced smile. "Sit down, and I'll pour you a cup."

Thomas pulled out a chair and sat at the head of the table, the legs scraping against the floor. Evelyn grabbed a mug from the cupboard and filled it, her hands steady despite the storm raging inside her.

As she placed the mug in front of him, she felt his eyes on her.

"You didn't sleep well," he said.

It wasn't a question.

Evelyn forced a laugh, brushing a stray curl from her face. "Too much on my mind, I guess. I was sure there were going to be more storms, and it must have worried me."

Thomas nodded, taking a sip of his coffee. "Roof held up through the last stretch of storms, at least."

She nodded, avoiding his gaze. The lie sat heavy on her tongue, bitterer than any truth could ever be.

After Thomas left for the fields, Evelyn sank into the chair across from his, her energy drained. She clasped her hands together on the table, her wedding band catching the light.

The guilt pressed down on her chest, constricting her breath. She loved Thomas in her own way. She respected him. He was a good man, steady and kind, a hard worker who had provided for her and Seth through the toughest of times. But what she felt for James was something else entirely.

With James, she was weightless, unguarded. The boundaries that hemmed her in—wife, mother, farmer's daughter—blurred and faded. But as much as she cherished those moments, they came at a cost. The lie she carried now stretched thin between her and Thomas, fragile as glass. One wrong move, one misstep, and it would shatter, cutting everyone she loved.

The back door creaked open, pulling her from her thoughts. Seth bounded in, cheeks flushed and hair sticking to his forehead.

"Ma, Mr. Thompson's got a new calf!" he said, grinning. "Says I can come help name her!"

Evelyn's heart dropped, but she smiled, smoothing his hair. "That's nice of him. Go wash up first, though."

Seth darted toward the washbasin, and Evelyn turned back to the table, gripping the edge. Her breaths came shallow, her mind racing. She couldn't deny her son the joy of the simple life they'd built, nor could she risk exposing the cracks she and James had carved into it.

But how long could she keep walking this tightrope? How long before the weight of it all became too much to bear?

Chapter Fifteen

Dear Evelyn

October 17, 1933

My Dearest Evelyn,

The days grow shorter now, the mornings heavy with mist, as if the world itself is mourning something lost. It was nearly a year ago that I stood by Margaret's grave, clutching our child's unused baby blanket close to my chest, the earth cold beneath my feet. I thought then that I would never feel warmth again, never know joy, never dare to hope. And yet, here I am, pen trembling in hand, pouring out my heart to you, the woman who has taught me how to live again.

How does one begin to describe a love that defies words and seems too vast for this world? Evelyn, you are the light in a life that has known too much shadow. Every time I see you—tending to your garden, brushing a strand of hair from your face, laughing in that quiet way of yours—it's as though the earth stands still, just for a moment. And yet, I know the weight you carry, the bonds that hold you fast to a life that cannot be ours.

I wish I could offer you a simple love free from shadows and secrets, but ours is not a world that allows such things. Still, I cannot help but dream of a life where we are free to walk hand in hand without fear of whispers, where I could lay my head beside yours at night and wake to the sight of you each morning. Forgive me for daring to imagine such a thing, for I know it can never be.

Sometimes, I wonder, Evelyn, if we were born at the wrong time. Perhaps in another life, in another place, we could have been together without question. I have thought—selfishly, I admit—of asking you to run away with me, to leave everything behind and start anew. But even as the thought tempts me, I know I could never truly ask it of you. To uproot your life, to turn your back on the family you hold so dear—it would be a cruelty I could not bear to inflict.

And yet, the idea of letting you go, of never feeling your hand in mine again, is a pain I cannot endure. The world may think me a fool, but I would rather have these stolen moments with you, fleeting though they may be, than a lifetime without you. If this love is a sin, then I shall gladly bear the weight of it.

I know the risk we take each time we meet, the danger that lurks in every glance, every touch. But Evelyn, I beg of you, do not let fear rob us of what little we can have. Say you will meet me again, if only for an hour, if only in the quiet shadows where no one can see. I need you more than I need air to breathe.

I have been thinking, my love, that we need a way to keep our words safe, a way to reach one another even when the risk feels too great. There is a crooked willow tree on the bend of Willow Branch Road, its trunk hollowed by age. I could place a small birdhouse there—simple and unassuming—where we might leave our letters for one another. A signal, perhaps, to let you know when I've left something: a ribbon tied to the branch or a wildflower tucked near its base. It is not much, I know, but it would mean we are not always waiting, hoping for a chance that may not come. What do you think, Evelyn? Could this be our refuge, small and secret, carved out of a world that would never understand? We could check it daily or as often as we can make our way to that special place.

Please, my love, do not think me selfish for asking this of you. I know I am asking for the impossible, but I am a man hopelessly in love, and reason has no place in a heart so full as mine. Whatever you decide, know that you are etched into me, as permanent as the rivers carving their way through these hills.

Yours, always and in every way,

James

Chapter Sixteen

The Whispers of Scandal

The morning frost clung to the windowpanes like lace, delicate but unyielding, as Evelyn sat on the edge of the worn oak chair in the kitchen. Her hands rested on the table, trembling ever so slightly, as though the weight of the secret inside her had already seeped into her bones. The mantel clock ticked steadily, a metronome for her racing thoughts.

It had been weeks since she first felt the changes in her body—little things at first, easily brushed aside as exhaustion or stress. But now, there was no denying it. Her dress, usually snug at the waist, felt tighter. The sickness came in waves each morning, relentless and insistent.

Her fingers pressed against her abdomen, the slight swell beneath her hand sending a complicated wave of emotion through her. She thought of James—how he had lost his child before it had even taken its first breath. What would it mean to give him this, something he had once dreamed of but could never have? The thought struck her with equal parts hope and dread. This child was a piece of him, of their love, undeniable proof of a bond that had transcended reason.

And yet, it was impossible. This life growing within her wasn't just a symbol of love but a harbinger of ruin. It wasn't hers to give, not to James, not to anyone. How could she reconcile the beauty of this child—a secret she longed to cherish—with the devastation its existence could bring? To her marriage, to the farm, to the fragile balance of lives built on sacrifice and duty?

Thomas's boots clomped on the porch outside, the sound of his approach jolting her back to reality. Evelyn stiffened, willing her body to stillness as he entered.

"Cold out there today," he said, pulling off his gloves and placing them near the stove. He gave her a quick smile, his face ruddy from the chill.

"Yes," Evelyn murmured, her voice thin.

Thomas poured himself a cup of coffee and settled into the chair across from her. His presence was solid, familiar, a foundation she'd built her life upon. And yet, the weight in her chest grew heavier under his gaze.

"You all right?" he asked, tipping his head to study her.

Evelyn swallowed hard, nodding too quickly. "Just tired. There's so much to do before winter sets in."

Thomas grunted in agreement, thankfully taking her words at face value. He drained his cup and rose, pressing a quick kiss to her temple before heading back out. The door closed behind him, and Evelyn exhaled a breath she didn't realize she'd been holding.

She moved to the window, staring out at the barren fields. The land that had anchored her now felt like a prison, every furrowed line a reminder of the life she was tied to.

Her hand returned to her abdomen, lingering there as her eyes filled with tears. This child was everything she could never give James and everything she couldn't take from Thomas. It was a cruel paradox—a symbol of love born from a connection she'd told herself was fleeting, now tied irrevocably to the choices she hadn't thought through.

How had she let it go this far? She had thought their love was a quiet refuge, a place to catch her breath in a life of endless responsibility. But now, it felt like she had drawn James into a storm neither of them could weather.

She turned from the window, clutching the edge of the sink for support as the truth swelled within her. She wanted to believe that love could be enough, that this child could be a blessing. But the world she lived in had no room for blessings born of stolen moments and whispered promises.

The truth was a seed planted deep inside her, growing with each passing day. Soon, it would show itself to the world, whether she was ready or not. And Evelyn wasn't sure if she'd ever be ready.

***

The house was unnervingly quiet, save for the faint crackle of the fire in the hearth. Evelyn stood near the mantle, her arms crossed tightly over her chest as if that could keep the truth from spilling out. The soft flicker of flames played across her face, but the warmth did little to ease the icy tension gripping her. She'd waited until after supper, after the dishes were washed and Thomas had settled into his chair, to summon the courage.

Now, as she heard his steady footsteps approaching the room, her heart threatened to pound out of her chest.

Thomas stopped in the doorway, his shadow stretching long across the floor. He glanced at her with mild curiosity, a single brow lifting. "You look like you've seen a ghost. What's got you so worked up?"

Evelyn turned to face him fully, her palms damp and trembling. "Thomas," she began, her voice wavering, "I need to talk to you about something... important."

He crossed the room and settled into his chair by the fire, leaning back with his usual air of calm practicality. "All right. I'm listening."

She couldn't help but wish he'd been this eager to hear her out months ago when she wanted to strengthen their marriage. If he had... would any of this have happened? She didn't know... but it was too late now. She had to face the music, as hard as it was going to be.

The words she'd rehearsed a hundred times dissolved on her tongue, leaving only the raw truth she could no longer contain. She sank into the chair across from him, clutching the fabric of her skirt. She wished she was anywhere but here, in another city, in another country, so far away that this farm didn't even register in her mind.

But she was sitting across from her husband, and now she had to tell him the hardest secret she'd ever had to keep... It came bursting out of her before she could worry about it anymore: "I'm pregnant."

Thomas didn't move, didn't even blink. For a moment, the only sound was the pop of a log in the fire. Then he exhaled a slow breath through his nose, his gaze settling on her with the weight of a man who'd spent his life reading storms before they arrived.

"Are you certain?" he asked, his voice level but edged with something unreadable.

Evelyn nodded, her throat too tight to speak.

He leaned forward, resting his elbows on his knees, his eyes fixed on the floor. "Well," he said finally, "I reckon congratulations are in order."

Her stomach twisted at the bitter humor in his tone. "Thomas, please... don't—"

"Don't what?" His gaze snapped to hers, sharp but not unkind. "Don't point out that this is as much a surprise to me as it is to you?

Or should I skip ahead to the part where I pretend not to know what this means?"

Evelyn's breath hitched. She couldn't bring herself to say his name—not here, not now. But she didn't have to. The silence between them was loud enough to speak for both of them.

Evelyn felt the room closing in around her, the air thick with a tension she could almost touch. She clutched the edge of the table to steady herself, her nails biting into the worn wood. The flickering lamplight cast shadows across Thomas's face, deepening the lines around his mouth and eyes. He looked older, wearier than she had ever noticed before, and it twisted something deep inside her.

"I'll ask you this once," Thomas said, his voice low, a razor's edge of calm that cut deeper than any shout could have. "Do you love him?"

The question hung in the air, heavy and damning. Evelyn's breath hitched, and she turned her head away, unable to meet his gaze. Her throat felt tight, the words lodged there like stones.

"It doesn't matter," she whispered, her voice barely audible.

"It matters to me," Thomas shot back, his voice cracking just slightly on the last word.

Evelyn looked at him then, her heart breaking at the raw hurt in his eyes. How had it come to this? She'd never wanted to hurt him, never wanted to destroy what they had built. But the truth was impossible to hide now.

"Thomas," she began, her voice trembling, "I never meant for this to happen. I made a mistake, a terrible mistake, and now—"

"And now you're carrying his child," he said, cutting her off. He leaned back in his chair, his hands gripping the armrests so tightly his knuckles turned white. The finality in his tone made her chest ache, a deep, gnawing pain that left her feeling hollow.

Evelyn pressed her hands against her stomach as if the gesture could shield her from the storm raging between them. She thought of James, of his gentle smile and the way his voice softened when he spoke to her. She loved him—she couldn't deny that, not to herself. But love hadn't been the plan, not for her and James. She had never intended for it to become this.

But Thomas—he had been her first love. She remembered the way he used to make her laugh until her sides ached, the way he'd pick wildflowers from the edge of the fields and tuck them behind her ear. She had loved him fiercely once, long before the weight of the farm, the bills and the endless grind of daily life had worn them down.

Tears spilled over, and she didn't bother to wipe them away. "I didn't want to hurt you," she said, her voice breaking. "I loved you, Thomas. I still—" She faltered, unsure if the words would mean anything to him now.

"Still what, Evelyn?" he asked, his voice hardening. "Still love me? After all this?"

Her breath hitched. Did she? She wasn't sure anymore. She wasn't sure of anything.

"I don't know," she admitted, the words cutting her as they left her lips. "I don't know what's true anymore. I just know I never stopped caring about you, and I never wanted to see you like this. I thought I could keep everything together, but I was wrong."

Thomas shook his head slowly, his jaw tight. "You thought you could have it both ways," he said bitterly. "Me and him. This life and... whatever you have with him. You're wrong, Evelyn. You can't."

The truth of his words hit her like a blow. She had been selfish, clinging to a love that had reignited something in her while trying to keep the fragile structure of her marriage intact. She thought of the man sitting across from her now, so broken yet so solid in his pain, and remembered the young man she had once adored.

"I loved you," she said quietly. "I loved you before all of this, before the farm, before everything got so... heavy. I remember who we used to be, Thomas. And I wish I could go back and hold on to that, but I didn't. I let it slip away."

Thomas's eyes narrowed, the hurt there replaced with something colder. "Maybe you should've told me that before you turned to him," he said.

"I tried!" Evelyn pleaded. "Don't you remember those nights I sent Seth to bed and made a special dinner just for us? Candles and the good china?"

Thomas had a blank expression, and Evelyn felt her pulse race with anger. He hadn't noticed what she'd tried to do, so why would she think talking to him about anything could have prevented this situation? But still, she felt shame, knowing it was much more her fault than his. She was the one who stepped outside of the marriage, of course. She bit her bottom lip hard to keep any more words from flying out; they wouldn't do any good now.

Thomas stared into the fire for a long moment, his jaw working as though chewing over the weight of all that had been said. Then he straightened, his shoulders squaring.

"We'll raise the child as ours," he said, his tone matter-of-fact.

Evelyn blinked, unsure she'd heard him correctly. "What?"

"I said we'll raise the child as ours," he repeated, his gaze meeting hers with an unflinching steadiness. "No one needs to know otherwise. Not the neighbors, not the church, not even the child. Your family has been on this land for generations, and I won't have our name dragged through the mud over one mistake."

Her breath caught in her throat. Relief and shame warred within her, leaving her unable to speak.

"This doesn't mean things go back to the way they were," Thomas continued, his voice softer but no less firm. "I'll do this for the sake of the family, for Seth, and for the innocent baby. But don't mistake this for forgiveness."

Evelyn swallowed hard, nodding as tears spilled down her cheeks. She didn't deserve forgiveness, and she knew it.

Thomas stood, his boots scuffing against the floor as he moved toward the door. Before he left, he paused, his hand resting on the door frame. "You should get some rest," he said, his voice void of warmth. "It's going to be a long winter."

And then he was gone, leaving Evelyn alone with the fire and the weight of what she'd set into motion.

***

The low murmur of voices followed Evelyn wherever she went as her belly started to expand throughout the winter. She had hoped people would be happy for her and Thomas and joked with Seth about becoming a big brother after so many years of being the one and only child. But it's like Evelyn wore the shame so openly that everyone could see it. They rarely saw Evelyn and Thomas together, so how would they blindly accept a new baby in that union? It was none of their business, of course, but in small, close-knit towns, that didn't matter. The whispers clung to the air like humidity after a late spring storm, unseen but impossible to ignore. She felt it in the quick glances exchanged between women at the mercantile, in the too-long pauses when she entered the church vestibule, and in the brittle smiles from neighbors who usually lingered to chat.

One morning, as she pulled Seth along by the hand into town, she could feel the weight of their eyes on her back. Her little boy chattered aimlessly about the calves in the barn, blissfully unaware of the currents swirling around them. Evelyn tried to focus on his words, to let their simplicity anchor her, but her grip on his hand tightened with every step.

At the general store, the bell above the door jangled as she walked in. Behind the counter, Mrs. Banks was busy measuring sugar into paper sacks. She glanced up, her face split into an automatic smile, but her eyes didn't quite reach Evelyn's.

"Morning, Evelyn," Mrs. Banks said, her voice warm enough but carrying a note of strained familiarity.

"Morning," Evelyn replied, setting her list on the counter. She knelt to adjust Seth's jacket, avoiding the woman's gaze.

The door opened behind her, and a gust of late winter wind swept in with it. She didn't turn, but the voices that followed were unmistakable—Mrs. Cline and Mrs. Barrett—the two self-appointed stewards of the town's moral compass.

"Oh, well, look who's here," Mrs. Cline said, her tone dripping with false sweetness.

Evelyn straightened and forced a smile, though her cheeks burned. "Good morning," she said, her voice steady despite the prickling heat climbing her neck.

Mrs. Barrett moved past her to inspect a shelf of canned goods, but not before murmuring something that sounded suspiciously like "shameless."

Evelyn's jaw tightened, her fists clenching as she pressed them against her sides. Seth tugged at her skirt. "Mama, can we get licorice?"

"Not today," she said gently, smoothing his hair. She had to stop and look at her hands, which were trembling.

The conversation at the counter continued, the two women pretending not to notice her but speaking loudly enough to ensure she heard every word.

"It's such a shame, isn't it?" Mrs. Cline said. "Certain people ought to think about the example they're setting, especially with a child involved."

Mrs. Barrett clucked her tongue. "You know how folks can be. They'll talk, whether there's truth to it or not."

Evelyn turned slowly to face them, her expression calm but her voice firm. "If either of you have something to say, you can say it to me directly."

The store fell silent, the only sound the soft rustle of the paper Mrs. Banks was folding. Mrs. Cline's face pinched, and she glanced at Mrs. Barrett, clearly not expecting Evelyn to address them outright.

"Oh, no one's accusing you of anything, dear," Mrs. Barrett said, her tone dripping with condescension. "We were just discussing how rumors get started, that's all."

Evelyn held her ground, her gaze steady. "Then perhaps you'd be better off discussing something else."

Seth tugged at her hand again. "Mama, I'm hungry."

She softened her grip and turned to Mrs. Banks. "I'll take what's on my list, please."

The tension in the room was palpable as Mrs. Banks hurried to fill the order. Evelyn stood tall, ignoring the whispers and the sideways glances from the other women.

When they stepped outside, the chill of the wind hit her like a slap. She took a deep breath, her shoulders stiff.

"Mama, are you mad?" Seth asked, looking up at her with wide, curious eyes.

"No, sweetheart," she said, squeezing his hand. "Just tired, that's all."

But she wasn't tired. She was exhausted—of the whispers, the eyes, the way people thought they could tear her apart with nothing more than pointed silence.

She glanced up the road toward Willow Branch, where James's farm sat just out of view. A familiar ache bloomed in her chest, one that she both welcomed and dreaded. She couldn't see him, couldn't risk adding fuel to the fire. Not now.

Instead, she gripped Seth's hand tighter and began the long walk home, her chin held high against the storm she could no longer escape.

***

The wooden pew beneath Evelyn's hands felt cold and unforgiving as she gripped it, her knuckles pale against the varnished oak. The murmurs behind her ebbed and flowed like the distant hum of cicadas, indistinct but persistent. She kept her gaze fixed forward, on the altar's flickering candles, their flames swaying gently with the draft that crept through the church.

Beside her, Thomas sat stiffly, his face a portrait of practiced in-difference. While he'd said they'd raise the baby together, he clearly didn't mean they'd act like a family unless they were at church. He took his meals in another room and never walked with Evelyn on the road, as if her shame cast such a wide net around her that there was no space for him anymore. But at church, they pretended all was well, as if the Lord didn't know the truth. At least James wasn't here to see them. He'd stopped attending after he lost his wife, as if his faith left along with her.

Seth squirmed between them, swinging his legs as his small hands fumbled with the hem of his coat. Evelyn reached over to still him, smoothing the fabric with a touch more force than necessary.

"Settle, Seth," she whispered, her voice tight.

"Yes, Mama," he said softly, his gaze dropping to the scuffed toes of his shoes.

The congregation rose as Reverend Markham entered, the organ groaning to life with a hymn Evelyn barely registered. She stood with the others, her chin lifted, and began to sing, though the words tasted like ash on her tongue.

She could feel their eyes without looking. The women in the row behind her leaned in close to one another, their whispers carrying even above the music. To Evelyn, they weren't words but accusations, a chorus of doubt and judgment.

The hymn ended, and they sat. The sermon began, a winding, fervent reminder of sin and redemption, and Evelyn fought the urge to shrink into herself. Instead, she straightened her back, folding her hands neatly in her lap.

"...and let us not forget," Reverend Markham's voice echoed through the rafters, "that the choices we make, even in secret, have consequences. For us, and for those we love."

A ripple of murmurs followed his words, subtle but unmistakable. Evelyn's stomach churned. She kept her eyes forward, refusing to glance around the room.

Thomas shifted beside her. It was barely perceptible, but she knew him well enough to sense the tension in his frame. They hadn't spoken about the whispers since they started. He didn't need to say anything; his silence was heavy enough.

When the service finally ended, Evelyn rose quickly, her hand firm on Seth's shoulder as they made their way down the aisle.

"Evelyn."

The voice stopped her cold. She turned slowly, her polite smile like a shield. Mrs. Cline stood there, flanked by Mrs. Barrett, both wearing their Sunday best and the thinly veiled satisfaction of women who lived for small-town intrigue.

"Mrs. Cline," Evelyn said smoothly, inclining her head.

"Lovely service today, wasn't it?" Mrs. Cline said, though her smile didn't reach her eyes.

"It was," Evelyn replied, her tone crisp.

"We've been meaning to ask," Mrs. Barrett interjected, her voice oozing with false sweetness, "how you've been managing things at the farm. With your condition and all, it must be such a challenge."

"We manage just fine," Evelyn said, her smile tightening.

"That's good to hear," Mrs. Cline said, drawing out the words. "It's important to set an example, especially for the little ones."

Evelyn's fingers curled into her skirt. She forced herself to nod. "I couldn't agree more."

Seth tugged at her hand, his wide eyes darting between the women. "Mama, can we go home now?"

"Yes," she said, her voice softening as she looked down at him. "We're going home."

Without waiting for another word, she turned and led Seth away, her heart pounding in her chest.

Outside, the air was brisk, and there was no sign of spring, which should be coming any day now. She breathed deeply, trying to push down the knot of anger and humiliation twisting inside her.

"Did I do something bad, Mama?" Seth asked, his small hand warm in hers.

"No, baby," she said quickly, crouching to meet his gaze. "You're perfect. Don't you worry about anything."

He nodded, though his brow furrowed in confusion. Evelyn smoothed his hair and stood, glancing toward the road toward home.

Thomas was already there, a vague shape in the distance. Well, if he wouldn't even wait for his wife and child to leave church, there was surely no way Evelyn could hope to squash the rumors any time soon. So much for acting like a complete family in public.

As she and Seth stepped into the road, Evelyn stared straight ahead, her head high, even as tears burned in her eyes. She wouldn't let them see her break. Not now. Not ever.

Chapter Seventeen

The Separation of Family

The air was heavy with the scent of lavender and lye soap as Evelyn gripped the edge of the bed frame, her knuckles turning white. The low hum of cicadas outside the open window mixed with the muffled murmurs of Mrs. Walker, the midwife, who moved with quiet efficiency around the room. The June heat clung to Evelyn's skin, soaking through her thin nightgown and plastering damp strands of hair to her forehead.

"One more, Evelyn," Mrs. Walker urged gently, her hands poised beneath the worn sheet that covered Evelyn's knees. "Just one good push now, sweetheart."

Evelyn bore down, her body straining with the effort. The room spun briefly, a haze of pain and exhaustion, until finally, the cry of a newborn split the air. She collapsed back against the pillows, chest heaving, as Mrs. Walker lifted the wailing infant into the dim light of the oil lamp.

"It's a boy," Mrs. Walker announced with a smile, her weathered face softening as she placed the child on Evelyn's chest. "A strong, healthy boy."

Evelyn stared at him, her breath catching. His skin was pink and slick, his tiny fists flailing as he screamed with all the strength his small body could muster. She reached out with trembling fingers to brush the wet curls on his head. Her heart ached, a tangle of love and guilt that she could barely untangle. He was beautiful, perfect even, but all she could see was James in the sharp slope of his nose, the delicate curve of his chin.

Thomas stood near the doorway, his broad shoulders tense as he watched. His face was unreadable, but his hands, calloused from years of working the fields, were clenched at his sides. He had been distant through the labor, pacing the hallway like a man bracing for a storm. Now, he stepped forward slowly, as though the space between them was an uncharted wilderness.

"Come, Thomas," Mrs. Walker said, motioning him over. "Your boy is here. See for yourself."

For a moment, he didn't move. Evelyn's heart twisted as she glanced up at him, the weight of what they both knew lying unspoken between them. Finally, he crossed the room, his boots heavy against the wooden floorboards, and leaned down to look at the baby. His expression softened, just barely, as he gazed at the child.

"Samuel," Evelyn said quietly, the name trembling on her lips. "His name is Samuel."

Thomas nodded, his jaw tightening. "Samuel," he echoed, his voice low and steady. He reached out, hesitating for a moment before brushing a finger against the baby's cheek. "He's... he's ours now."

Evelyn closed her eyes, tears slipping free despite her best efforts to hold them back. His words, though kind on the surface, carried the weight of a promise they both knew would never be entirely true. Samuel was their son, yes, but he would always be James's, too, a fact that neither time nor pretense could erase.

As Mrs. Walker bustled about, cleaning and tidying, Evelyn watched Thomas lift Samuel into his arms. The sight brought a fresh wave of emotion, sharp and bittersweet. He cradled the baby awkwardly at first but then with a tenderness she hadn't seen in years. It reminded her of the man he had been before the stress of the crash and the struggles with the farm, before... James.

"Do you want me to take him?" Evelyn asked softly, her voice tentative.

"No," Thomas said quickly, his eyes never leaving the baby's face. "I'll hold him. I'll let Seth see him in a moment."

She watched them together, father and son, in a tableau that should have brought her peace but instead felt like a knife twisting in her heart. Samuel had no idea of the life he was entering, the web of lies, love, and sacrifice that had brought him into being.

As Thomas swayed gently, murmuring something low and soothing, Evelyn turned her face to the window. The fields outside shimmered in the moonlight, wide and empty, like the life she and Thomas had once shared. She thought of James, of the way his hand had lingered on hers the last time they spoke, his voice thick with longing as he told her he understood.

She loved Samuel with every fiber of her being. But as she watched Thomas hold him, his expression a mix of love and sorrow, she wondered if she would ever forgive herself for the cost of that love—for the secret that would always linger, unspoken, in the space between them.

***

The sun dipped low over the hills, casting a warm, golden glow across the fields. James stood at the edge of his property, just beyond the willow trees that gave Willow Branch Road its name. From here, the view of the Harris farm was both familiar and agonizing—a tableau of life he couldn't fully claim.

He shifted his weight, the dry grass crunching beneath his boots, as he leaned against the fencepost. In the yard below, Evelyn moved with easy grace, her hair catching the last light of day. He could see the bundle in her arms, but that wasn't enough to satisfy his curiosity.

He's mine, James thought bitterly, gripping the fencepost so hard the rough wood bit into his palm. And he doesn't even know.

Thomas appeared in the doorway of the barn, wiping his hands on a rag. He called something to Evelyn, and she smiled up at him, though the curve of her lips looked more weary than joyful.

James turned away sharply, his throat constricting. He couldn't watch Thomas like this, couldn't stand the easy way he reached for the baby in Evelyn's arms as if he had every right in the world to call him son.

The ache in James's chest wasn't new—it had lived there since the day Evelyn told him the truth. She had come to him trembling, her words rushing out in broken fragments. She was pregnant. The baby was his. And there was nothing they could do about it.

"Thomas will raise him," she had said, her voice thick with tears. "It's the only way."

James had nodded then, though every part of him had screamed to argue. To fight. To beg her to leave, to come to him instead. But he had stayed silent because he understood that appearances mattered. The farm mattered. The family name mattered. And he, the widowed neighbor with dirt under his nails and a broken heart, could never offer her what she needed.

Now, he lived with the consequences of that silence every day. He stayed in the shadows, keeping the secret that bound him to Evelyn in ways no one could see.

Does she think of me when she looks at him? James wondered. Does she see me in his eyes?

He knew Evelyn loved Samuel fiercely, the way she loved Seth, her firstborn—with all the tenderness of a mother protecting her child. And he knew she loved Thomas, too, in her own quiet, dutiful way. But there had been something between them once—something that burned hotter and brighter than either of them had expected. He still felt it, even now, a slow and steady flame that refused to die.

But love, he had learned, wasn't always enough.

With a heavy sigh, James stepped away from the fence. The house was calling him, and the chores he had neglected in favor of this self-inflicted torment were waiting to be finished. He took one last look at the Harris farm, at the life that could have been his, before turning away. The shadows lengthened around him as he walked back toward his own empty home.

**

The house felt too small for the life it held, too quiet in a way that made Evelyn's chest ache with every breath. She sat by the window, her hands folded tightly in her lap, watching the sun dip beneath the hills. The heat of the day still lingered in the air, but it did little to warm the cold knot that had settled in her stomach.

Samuel's cries echoed through the house, sharp and urgent, as Thomas stepped into the room, his face tight. His brows furrowed with that all-too-familiar weariness. She could feel the strain between them, the weight of secrets buried too deep to dig back up.

"I'll go," Evelyn said softly, but Thomas shook his head, his lips tight.

"No, I've got him," he muttered. He turned toward the sound of their son's distress, each step heavy with something that wasn't just exhaustion.

Evelyn watched him leave, a hollow ache widening in her chest. It wasn't the first time he'd taken care of Samuel instead of her, but every time, it felt like a little piece of her heart broke off.

She stood up and crossed the room, her movements slow, deliberate. A gust of wind greeted her as she opened the door, cool and bitter. She stepped out onto the porch, feeling the evening air tug at her skin.

James's house now seemed a thousand miles away, separated by more than just the space between their two properties. She could still see him—his face hard and withdrawn while he worked on his own farm, so close yet so far away from hers.

She'd thought time would heal the cracks between them, but instead, the silence had deepened. The love she'd felt for him, the pull she couldn't resist, seemed to suffocate her in ways she couldn't explain. The loss was almost too much, despite the joy Samuel brought to her life.

Her heart was heavy as she walked down the steps of the porch and toward the fence that divided her life from his. She thought she might hear his footsteps on the dirt road that ran between their properties, the creak of his boots as he approached. But there was nothing.

Not even the sound of the wind. Just the far-off hum of crickets.

She stood at the edge of the fence for a long time, staring at the silhouette of his house through the trees, wondering if James was doing the same thing. Waiting. For what? For things to change? For everything to fall into place in a way that could never be fixed?

In the weeks since Samuel had been born, she'd seen him—seen James—less and less. And every time, it felt like something in him was slipping away. The guilt gnawed at her. She had chosen this life—chosen Thomas despite the truth of what she and James had shared. She had chosen to give up everything she'd wanted for something that wasn't even hers anymore.

Evelyn turned away from the fence, walking back toward the house, where Thomas was rocking Samuel to sleep. The boy's cries had quieted, replaced by the soft cooing of a lullaby she had never sung.

The door clicked shut behind her as she entered the living room. Thomas sat in his chair, the one by the fire, with Samuel cradled against his chest. The sight should have been comforting. It should have felt like home. But Evelyn couldn't help but wonder if this was really her home at all.

"He's asleep," Thomas said quietly, his voice distant, almost defeated. "Seth, too, already in bed."

Evelyn didn't answer, unable to find the words. She sat across from him, the silence stretching between them like a gulf they were too afraid to cross.

After a long pause, Thomas spoke again, his voice rough, as though it had been too long since he last allowed himself to feel anything.

"Do you ever think about him?" His eyes flicked up to meet hers. His jaw tightened.

Evelyn's breath caught in her throat. Her fingers gripped the arm of the chair, her knuckles pale. She didn't have to answer. He knew. And the fact that he had asked—that he had brought it up—made her heart ache all over again.

"Why would you ask me that?" she whispered, barely loud enough for him to hear.

Thomas's face displayed a sadness she couldn't bear to look at. He had found an answer in what she diplomatically thought was a non-answer. He stood abruptly, lifting Samuel carefully, his expression unreadable.

"I'll take him to bed," he said.

Evelyn nodded, but she didn't follow him. Instead, she remained in her chair, staring at the empty space where Thomas had been, feeling the weight of a life that wasn't quite hers, a life that never would be.

When the door to the boys' bedroom closed softly behind Thomas, Evelyn let out a breath she hadn't known she'd been holding. She had to fight the tears that threatened to spill. But what good would they do? What good was anything when all she could feel was the emptiness that settled in her chest like a stone?

The love she had for James, for her sons, for Thomas—it was all twisted, all bound up in knots she couldn't untangle. And the harder she tried, the deeper they dug in.

She closed her eyes, leaning back into the chair. Somewhere in the distance, she could hear the wind picking up again, but this time, it felt colder. And she knew, deep down, that the winds had shifted. It seemed like the silence between them, between her and James, wasn't going to break. Not now. Not ever.

***

Evelyn stood by the window, staring out at the moonlit fields. The night was still, except for the rustling of the trees in the breeze. The house behind her was quiet, as it always was now—silent except for the muffled sounds of Thomas's heavy breathing as he slept. It had been like this for months, years, really—him, distant and heavy with the unspoken truths, and her, aching with the hollow space between them. She knew Samuel wouldn't change things, but she had hoped that something would give, that somehow things would become a little softer between them.

She squinted into the darkness, trying to see if... yes, that shadow, that figure. It was James! Before she knew what she was doing, she tiptoed across the room and opened the back door. The night air hit her like a cold kiss, and she hurried outside and then started running once she was in the field.

"James," she called as loudly as she dared. There was no one else for miles, and Thomas was deeply asleep, but she still worried about people hearing.

"Evelyn," James said, his voice a low rasp, as though speaking her name was a weight in itself. His face was half-shadowed, his broad shoulders hunched against the chill. His hands were at his sides, clenched into fists that trembled ever so slightly.

Suddenly, Evelyn didn't know what to say. She had been thinking of him nonstop for weeks, feeling the pain of being without him. But now, standing in front of him, she felt lost.

"How's Samuel?" he asked quietly.

"Sleeping," Evelyn whispered, pulling her shawl tighter around her shoulders.

"We shouldn't be here," James said, his words tight. "But..."

"I know," she interrupted softly. She couldn't bear to hear him say it, to hear the weight of the words that would never leave them: that Samuel, their child, would never be his. That the world would never know the truth of him, never know the love they shared in secret.

She stepped closer, her fingers brushing against his rough palm. It was a fleeting touch, but the warmth of it burned through her like fire. She could feel the pain between them, the yearning, the longing for something they could never have.

"James," she whispered, her voice trembling. "It's too hard."

"I know," he said, his voice breaking for a brief second. "I thought it would get easier, Evelyn. But it hasn't. Every day, it gets worse."

She nodded, swallowing the lump in her throat. "We can't keep doing this. It's killing me."

He took a step back, the movement sharp and desperate. "But we don't have a choice. There's no way out, not for either of us. I can't... I can't lose him. And you can't lose your family."

The words stung more than she expected because he was right. She had made her choice when she married Thomas, when she became his wife, his partner, and they had Seth. And yet, she had made another, harder choice when she decided to keep Samuel, to raise him with Thomas as his father. But she had never been prepared for the depth of what it would cost her. She had never been prepared for the ache of watching the man she loved from afar, knowing they would never truly be together.

"James, please," she said, her voice breaking. "I want more than this. I want us... I wish we could be a family, to raise him together. But we can't, can we? Not here. Not now."

James shook his head slowly, his eyes dark with something between regret and resignation. He closed his eyes briefly, his lips pressed into a tight line. When he opened them again, there was a quiet finality in his gaze.

"No," he said softly, his voice steady but full of grief. "We can't. I... I've never wanted anything more, Evelyn. But we can't have it. Not in this world."

She reached for him, pulling him close, her hands clutching the fabric of his coat, pulling him into her as though she could somehow bind them together, somehow make it so that this wasn't just a painful memory to carry.

"I wish things were different," she whispered against his chest, her breath ragged.

"I do too," he answered, his voice thick with emotion.

But there was nothing left to say, not anymore. The words that needed to be said would never be spoken, and the life they both dreamed of would never come to pass. They were trapped in the spaces between what was and what could never be.

James stepped away from her slowly, his hands lingering for a moment on her arms before he turned toward his house. Evelyn watched him, her heart breaking with every step he took away from her, knowing that when they parted tonight, they would be further apart than ever before.

"I'll see you again," he said, his voice barely audible.

Evelyn didn't answer. She couldn't. She just stood there in the dark, watching him disappear into the night, knowing that every time he left, it would hurt just a little more.

Chapter Eighteen

Dear James

September 12, 1934

My Dearest James,

I sit here tonight, by the dim light of the oil lamp, unable to stop my mind from racing with the thoughts that have weighed me down for so long. Every time I close my eyes, I hear Samuel's soft breathing, feel the warmth of his tiny hand in mine, and I think of you. I think of all that should be and all that will never be. And it tears at my heart, James. It tears at me in ways I cannot explain.

I hate it. I hate that you are not here with him. I hate that you cannot be the father you should be, that you cannot raise him as your own, as you so desperately want to. How cruel it feels to carry this child in my arms, to nurse him and watch him grow, knowing that you will never get to do the same.

Sometimes, I wonder if you ever look at him from a distance, from the shadows, and wonder who he might have been if we had been able to make a life together. I wonder if he ever reminds you of your own lost dreams, the things we've both given up for the sake of this farce we're living. You are his father, and yet you are forced to live as if you are nothing more than a stranger.

I've enclosed the letter I wrote to you in July of 1932. I never sent it, but I know I must now. I know you'll need to read it now, just as you need to know that I have loved you from the moment I first laid eyes on you. Every day, I have carried that love with me like a secret burden, like a treasure I could never share with the world. I pray that you understand, that you know the depth of my feelings, and that even though we cannot be together, my heart has always been yours.

I've kept all my feelings locked away, buried beneath the duties of a wife, a mother, and a neighbor. But in my heart, I am still the woman who would have run to you had the world allowed it.

It is cruel, James. So cruel. I know this situation is eating us both alive, but there is nothing I can do. I have tried. I have tried to be patient, to be strong for you, for Samuel, for Thomas, even for the life that we built together, but it is a strain I can no longer bear without breaking. My heart is so full of sorrow, and I know you feel it too. How could you not? The silence between us is like an ocean, and every day, it grows wider, deeper, more impossible to cross.

I dream of a different life, a life where we could stand together, raise Samuel without shame, without fear of the secrets that lurk in the dark. I wish for a world where you could be his father without apology, where no one would question our love, where we could live freely. I yearn for it with every fiber of my being, but I know it will never happen. The world we live in is too small for dreams like ours and too cold to hold the warmth we could have shared.

I want to fix this, James. I want to take away the pain, to make it so that we can hold our son together so that you can kiss his brow and know him as your own. But I am powerless, and that is what kills me most. I am bound to a life I did not choose, one where the love we share must be hidden away, like a guilty secret. But know this: that love has never faltered. It is as real as the earth beneath our feet, as constant as the moonlight that falls over these fields. It is not a passing thing, not something that can be swept away by time or circumstance.

And so, we continue as we must, each of us playing our parts, pretending in front of the world but holding the truth in the silence between us. It is the only way we can survive this, the only way we can protect our hearts from the weight of the life we cannot have.

I will never stop loving you, James. And I hope, one day, when time has passed and the world has moved on, you will remember me with the same tenderness that I carry for you. Perhaps then, we will be free—free to love without fear, without regret.

Until then, know that every part of me aches for you. I am with you in every moment, in every thought, in every prayer.

Yours, now and always,

Evelyn

P.S. The letter included here that I wrote you in 1932—know that it was true then, and it is true now. I have never stopped loving you.

Chapter Nineteen

The Stolen Moments

The crisp scent of autumn hung heavy in the air as Evelyn made her way through the sugar maple grove bordering her farm. The hem of her dress caught on brambles, but she didn't slow, clutching Samuel tighter against her chest. His breath puffed soft and rhythmic against her collarbone; his tiny hand curled around a strand of her hair. She adjusted the shawl draped around them both, shielding his fragile body from the cool breeze.

Ahead, the clearing came into view, dappled in golden light filtering through the thinning canopy. James stood there, leaning against the old oak, his posture still and waiting, save for the restless movement of his hands. When he saw her, he straightened, the tension in his shoulders easing just slightly. His face softened in a way it never did around others, a flicker of joy tempered by restraint.

Evelyn stepped into the clearing, her heart both leaping and sinking at the sight of him. "I can't stay long," she said quietly, more an apology than a greeting.

James nodded, his eyes fixed on the bundle in her arms. "I'm just glad you came," he murmured, his voice low and rough with emotion.

Evelyn carefully lowered Samuel into his arms, her fingers brushing against his as they passed the child between them. James cradled his son as if he were made of spun glass, his weathered hands incongruously gentle against the baby's soft skin. Samuel stirred, blinking up at him with drowsy curiosity. James let out a shaky breath and smiled, though it didn't quite reach his eyes.

"He's getting so big," he said, his voice barely above a whisper. "I feel like I missed half of him already."

Evelyn sank onto the blanket James had spread across the grass, its edges slightly tinged with dampness from the morning dew. She watched as James sat beside her, Samuel still in his arms, staring at the baby with the kind of longing that broke her heart anew each time she saw it.

"You haven't missed anything that matters," she said, though her voice faltered as she spoke. "He's here now."

James chuckled softly, a bitter edge to the sound. "But for how long? How many more stolen moments like this before it's too dangerous, before someone notices?"

Evelyn swallowed hard, the weight of his words pressing down on her chest. "I don't know," she admitted, her gaze dropping to the crumpled leaves at her feet. "I just know that this—these moments—they're all I can give you. They're all I have to give."

James fell silent, his head bowing as he pressed a kiss to Samuel's forehead. The baby gurgled, reaching up with a chubby hand to grab at the coarse fabric of James's shirt. James let out a breath that hitched midway, his eyes glistening as he fought to compose himself.

"He has your eyes," he said after a long pause, his voice thick with emotion. "And the way he smiles—it's like he knows, Evelyn. Like he knows me, even if I'm not allowed to be what I should be."

Evelyn leaned forward, her hand brushing lightly against his arm. "He'll always know you," she said fiercely. "Even if he doesn't know how, he'll feel it. I'll make sure of that."

James looked at her then, and for a moment, the sorrow and frustration in his expression gave way to something softer. "You always say the right thing," he murmured. "Even when it's impossible."

She wanted to argue, to say that nothing about this was right, that every step they took deeper into this secret was another wound neither of them could heal. But instead, she smiled faintly, her hand lingering on his arm.

The quiet stretched between them, broken only by the rustle of the wind through the trees and the soft coos of the baby in James's lap. Evelyn watched as he rocked Samuel gently, his movements instinctive, natural. For a moment, it was easy to imagine a different life—a life where they could be together, where Samuel's laugh would fill their home, and James could hold his son without fear.

But then the wind shifted, carrying the faint echo of a distant church bell from town, and reality came rushing back. Evelyn rose reluctantly, brushing leaves from her skirt. "I have to go," she said, her voice thick with regret.

James hesitated, his arms tightening protectively around Samuel. He stood slowly and handed the baby back to her, his movements heavy with reluctance. "Take care of him," he said softly, his eyes locked on hers. "And take care of yourself, too."

Evelyn nodded, unable to speak past the lump in her throat. She clutched Samuel close and turned away, heading back toward the farm without looking back. But as she walked, she felt James's gaze on her, as tangible as a touch, and she knew that the ache in her chest would stay with her long after she returned home.

***

The late afternoon sun bathed the fields in hues of amber and gold as Evelyn balanced Samuel on her hip, his chubby fist tangled in the fringe of her shawl. The autumn air had a crispness that hinted at the colder months ahead, but the warmth of the sun lingered, softening the edges of the chill. Evelyn glanced toward the barn, where Thomas was repairing a section of fencing. Beyond it, past the dirt road and the familiar sway of willow branches, James' silhouette appeared.

He carried a bundle of firewood in his arms, his stride steady as he approached the edge of their property. Her pulse quickened, though she kept her face neutral as if she hadn't noticed him at all. Samuel fussed in her arms, kicking his legs.

"Patience, little one," she murmured, shifting him so he could see more of the yard.

James stopped a few paces from the fence, carefully setting down the wood. He straightened and offered a small wave. Evelyn hesitated, then nodded in return, her heart tightening. He shouldn't be here. But, of course, he wasn't here—he was at the edge of his own property. There was nothing improper about it, not on the surface.

"Afternoon, Evelyn," he called, his voice carrying easily across the still air.

"Afternoon," she replied, adjusting Samuel on her hip.

"Thomas keeping busy?" James asked, leaning casually on the top rail of the fence.

"As always." Evelyn steadied Samuel in her arms as he reached out for a leaf, his tiny fingers closing around the brittle stem. "He's fixing the east fence. Some of the cows broke through last week."

James nodded, his gaze dropping to Samuel. The boy's round cheeks were flushed pink from the chill, his hazel eyes alight with the wonder of everything around him. A small smile touched James' lips. "Looks like someone's already getting to know the land."

Evelyn tensed but forced herself to stay calm. "He's curious about everything," she said softly. "Keeps me running in circles."

James' smile widened. He crouched down, resting his forearms on his knees. "Hello there, fella," he said, his tone low and warm. "What've you got there? A treasure?"

Samuel looked up at him, blinking, then held out the leaf proudly. James chuckled. "That's a good find," he said. "Bet your mama'll press that one in a book for you."

The casual way he said it, as if they were any two neighbors chatting over the fence, made Evelyn's throat tighten. Samuel reached out with his tiny hand, and James extended his own hand carefully, letting Samuel's fingers wrap around one of his.

The sight made Evelyn's chest ache. She could see the tenderness in James' expression, the quiet yearning he masked with a practiced ease. Samuel giggled, tugging on James' finger, and James chuckled softly, letting the boy test his strength.

"He's strong," James said, glancing up at her. "Got a grip like a mule."

Evelyn managed a faint smile, though her voice was steady when she spoke. "He'll need to be, growing up here."

James looked at the boy, his smile fading just slightly. "He's got good hands," he said, almost to himself. "Steady. Quick to learn, I'd bet."

He straightened, stepping back as if realizing he'd lingered too long. "I'll let you get back," he said quickly, his tone polite again. He glanced at Samuel one last time, his expression softening.

Evelyn lifted her hand in a wave, her throat too tight to speak. She watched as James picked up the firewood and turned back toward his own home, his steps slow and deliberate. Samuel babbled, tugging at the collar of her dress, and she held him close.

She stayed there long after James had disappeared from view, the sun dipping lower and casting long shadows across the yard. Samuel rested his head on her shoulder, his small body warm against hers, but Evelyn felt cold.

In these moments, she saw everything she had gained—and everything James had lost.

***

The lantern's weak glow barely cut through the shadows of the barn, casting flickering light over the hay-strewn floor. Evelyn stood just inside the door; her breath caught in her throat as she listened for any sign of movement beyond the creaking boards beneath her feet. The stillness of the night, broken only by the occasional rustle of a restless animal, made her pulse race all the more. Each sound could be Thomas stirring in the house or one of the neighbors passing by on the road, a witness to something that could never be undone.

Then came the soft crunch of boots on gravel, and her heart leaped into her throat. James stepped into the barn, his hat pulled low against the chill. His eyes met hers, and the tension in her chest loosened—just for a moment. He closed the door behind him quietly, leaning back against it, his broad shoulders slumping as though he were setting down a heavy burden.

"Evelyn," he said, her name a whisper that carried more weight than any declaration.

"You shouldn't have come," she replied, her voice steady despite the whirlwind inside her. "Thomas has been asking questions."

James's jaw tightened, and he took a step closer. "And yet, here you are, waiting."

Evelyn looked away, the truth in his words cutting deeper than she wanted to admit. The space between them seemed insurmountable and unbearably small all at once. "I don't know how much longer I can keep doing this," she said, her arms wrapping around herself as though to shield against the storm within. "Every time we meet, I think—this could be the moment we're found out."

He reached her in two strides, his hands gentle as they settled on her shoulders. "Do you think I don't feel it too? Every time I see Samuel..." His voice broke, and he paused, his fingers tightening ever so slightly. "I see the boy I'll never really get to know. The son who'll never call me his father. And it kills me, Evelyn."

Her throat ached with the weight of unshed tears. "He doesn't understand yet. He's too young to know... but he loves you, James. He lights up every time you're near."

"And when he's older?" James asked, his voice hoarse. "When he looks back and wonders why I was always just the kind neighbor? Why I didn't fight harder?"

Evelyn shook her head, stepping back and creating a fragile space between them. "Because it's not just about us. It's about protecting him, protecting Thomas, protecting the family. If people found out—" Her voice cracked, and she pressed her hand to her mouth, forcing herself to breathe. "This would ruin everything."

James exhaled sharply, his hands falling to his sides. "I hate this," he said, his voice low, angry. "I hate sneaking around like criminals. I hate pretending Samuel is nothing more than a neighbor's boy. I hate that you and I only get fragments of a life together."

She reached out, her fingers brushing his sleeve. "You think I don't hate it too? That I don't lie awake at night wondering if this is worth it? But then I think about how much worse it would be if I couldn't see you at all."

His eyes softened, and for a moment, the weight of their circumstances seemed to dissipate. He stepped closer again, his forehead resting against hers. "You're stronger than I am," he said softly. "You have to be."

"No," she whispered, her voice trembling. "I'm just as weak. That's why I'm here."

For a long moment, neither of them moved. The barn seemed to hold its breath with them, the world outside their fragile bubble of stolen time. But then James straightened, his hands falling away. "We can't stay long," he said, his tone steady, though his eyes betrayed his lingering anguish. "I'll walk you back. If anyone sees—"

"No one will," Evelyn interrupted, her voice firmer than she felt. "We've been careful."

James nodded, but the doubt lingered in his expression. "One day, Evelyn, we'll run out of careful."

She didn't respond. Instead, she turned toward the door, her shoulders squared even as her heart ached. She could feel James just behind her, his presence as steady as the love that both bound and tormented them. Each step back to the house felt like crossing a battlefield, every shadow a threat. But when they reached the edge of the barn, she paused, turning to look at him one last time.

"Goodnight, James," she said softly, the words weighted with everything she couldn't say.

"Goodnight, Evelyn," he replied, his voice barely more than a breath.

And then he was gone, disappearing into the darkness as she slipped back toward the house, where Samuel and Thomas waited in blissful, fragile ignorance.

Chapter Twenty

The Enduring Passion

The crisp air of late December clung to Evelyn's cheeks as she trudged across the frost-covered field, her arms wrapped tightly around a basket of firewood. The farm was quiet, save for the occasional groan of the wind and the far-off bark of a dog. Her breath came in visible puffs, mingling with the smoke that spiraled from the farmhouse chimney behind her. Ahead, the barren trees of Willow Branch Road stood like silent sentinels, their dark branches etched against the gray sky.

She paused at the edge of the field, glancing toward the narrow, winding path that led to James' farm. How many times had she walked that road under cover of darkness? How many nights had she pressed herself against him, her heart racing with the thrill and fear of it all? Even now, the thought of him sent warmth spiraling through her as if he had kindled a fire deep within her that could not be extinguished.

Evelyn's fingers tightened on the basket handle as she turned back toward the house. The risk of sneaking away tonight was too great.

Thomas was inside, reading to Seth by the fire, and Samuel was playing on the rug at their feet. Still, her mind lingered on James, as it always did. She could picture him now, alone in his barn, mending tack or stacking hay, his strong hands moving with the quiet precision she had always admired. She wondered if he thought of her, too, in these stolen hours between their carefully orchestrated meetings.

The farm was alive with the necessities of winter, the days consumed by feeding livestock and preparing for spring planting. Evelyn threw herself into the work, but even as she moved through the familiar routines, her thoughts often drifted to James.

He was so different from her father and her husband—steady but not unyielding, kind without being weak. There was a gentleness to him that belied his rugged exterior, and it had drawn her to him from the start. She remembered when she had first seen him after his wife and newborn had died, his grief etched so deeply into his features that it had taken her breath away. It was that grief, she realized now, that had connected them so strongly. She had wanted to ease his pain, to give him some part of herself that might help him heal. She hadn't known then how deeply she would come to love him or how impossible it would be to let him go.

Though the world outside was frosted over, her passion for James had only grown warmer and stronger. Despite the short days and sky darkening so early, she often caught herself glancing toward Willow Branch Road, her heart quickening at the thought of seeing him again.

One evening, when it was as black as midnight by just five o'clock, she found herself bundled up and walking the familiar path to his farm. The air smelled of freshly turned earth, and the soft hum of crickets filled the night.

James was waiting for her at the edge of the barn, his figure outlined against the glow of a lantern inside. When he saw her, his face broke into a quiet smile, and the sight of it made her heart ache with something too deep for words.

"You shouldn't have come," he said softly, though his arms opened to her all the same.

"I couldn't stay away," she admitted, stepping into his embrace. His warmth surrounded her, and for a moment, the world fell away.

They stood there for what felt like hours, neither of them speaking. The weight of their secrets hung between them, unspoken but understood. Yet, in that moment, none of it mattered. The only thing that mattered was the way his arms felt around her, the steady beat of his heart beneath her cheek.

"I wish things could be different," she whispered at last, her voice barely audible over the sound of the wind. "I wish we could be together without all this... hiding."

James tilted her chin up, his gaze steady and full of unspoken promises. "Evelyn, I'd wait a lifetime for the chance to be with you. But until then, I'll take whatever time I can get."

His words wrapped around her like a balm, soothing the ache in her chest. As the first stars began to appear in the night sky, she knew that no matter the cost, she would never stop loving him. The fire he had kindled within her burned as fiercely as ever, and it would carry her through the long, uncertain days ahead.

***

The Christmas tree in the corner of the parlor shimmered with strands of tinsel that caught the warm glow of the lantern light. Evelyn adjusted one of the ornaments, her hands trembling slightly. Samuel sat on the floor beside the tree, his face alight with wonder as he admired his newest treasure: a wooden rocking horse. It was a handsome thing, painted a soft brown with a yarn mane and a carefully carved saddle, its rockers smooth and polished.

"Do you like it, Samuel?" James asked, crouching beside the boy with a quiet smile.

Samuel nodded eagerly, his little hands gripping the reins as he climbed aboard. He rocked back and forth, giggling at the way the horse swayed beneath him. Evelyn's heart twisted at the sight of James watching Samuel with such tenderness. For a moment, it was as though time had stilled, and they were just a family—a fleeting, impossible dream.

Thomas stood by the doorway, his hands shoved into his pockets. His expression was neutral, but Evelyn could see the tension in his jaw, the way his shoulders seemed rigid beneath his worn flannel shirt.

"You did fine work on that horse, James," Thomas said evenly. "Samuel seems to like it well enough."

"Glad he does," James replied, standing and brushing his hands on his trousers. "He deserves something special for Christmas." His tone was light, but the words carried weight. Evelyn glanced away, her chest tightening.

"Well," Thomas said after a beat, "you'll have to show me how you managed that saddle sometime. Clean craftsmanship."

Evelyn forced a smile, stepping forward to gather the discarded ribbons and wrapping paper from the floor. "Samuel, why don't you ride your horse in the kitchen for a bit? That way, we can clean up in here before Seth comes home from school."

Samuel obeyed, eagerly dragging the rocking horse across the floorboards with a clatter. When he was out of earshot, the room fell into a heavy silence. James tipped his hat to Thomas, nodded once to Evelyn, and excused himself to leave.

The moment the latch clicked shut, Thomas exhaled sharply, the neutrality vanishing from his face. "Evelyn," he said, his voice low but sharp, "this has to stop."

She turned toward him, her hands still clutching the ribbons. "What do you mean?"

"You know what I mean." His blue eyes bore into hers, the calmness of his earlier demeanor gone. "That man has no place coming here with gifts for Samuel like he's... like he's—" Thomas broke off, shaking his head. "I claimed him as mine, Evelyn. I've done everything you asked. I've loved that boy, and I've never said a word about... about what we both know."

Her throat tightened. "Thomas, he wasn't—"

"I know exactly what he was doing," Thomas interrupted. "He's marking his place in Samuel's life, and I won't have it. Not in my house."

She bit her lip, her heart aching at the anger in his voice. "He's not trying to take anything from you," she said softly. "He's just—"

"Don't make excuses for him," Thomas snapped. Then, just as quickly, he softened, the tension in his shoulders sagging. He sighed, running a hand through his hair. "Look, you've got to think about how this looks—to me, to Seth, to Samuel, to the rest of the world. This... arrangement can't last forever."

Evelyn stood rooted in place, her mind racing. She had always known this moment would come, had always known that asking Thomas to raise Samuel as his own would carry a cost. And yet, hearing the pain in his voice now, she felt the full weight of what she had done.

"I don't want to hurt you," she said finally, her voice barely above a whisper.

Thomas looked at her for a long moment, his expression unreadable. "Then don't," he said simply, before turning and walking out of the room.

Evelyn sank into the nearest chair, her hands trembling as she smoothed the ribbon across her lap. Outside, she could hear the faint sound of James' truck starting up, the engine rumbling as it pulled away down Willow Branch Road.

She closed her eyes, torn between the two men who had claimed pieces of her heart. One she owed everything and one she could never truly have. For now, she would have to play it safe to keep the peace—for Thomas, for Seth and Samuel, and for herself. But deep in her heart, she knew the fire that burned for James would never fully die.

***

The kitchen smelled of fresh bread, and the faint tang of wood polish as Evelyn moved about the small, sunlit space. She kept her hands busy, wiping the already spotless counter, her heart thudding against her ribs. The little wooden trinket box sat on the edge of the table where she could glance at it every so often. Having it near made it seem as though it radiated heat, as though it might catch fire from her guilt and desire alone.

The box was simple but exquisite, carved from walnut with delicate heart-shaped curves. Its lid fit perfectly, the edges sanded smooth, the whole thing small enough to sit unnoticed on the palm of her hand. She hadn't asked James for it; it had simply appeared in her hands last night as the moon cast long shadows across the fields. He had pressed it into her palm, his fingers brushing hers, and whispered, "For the things you can't say aloud."

She had cried later that night, alone in her room. But she took it from her hiding spot on her dresser after Thomas went out to the fields, kept it tucked in her apron pocket as she baked bread, finally putting it on the table so she could look at it while she cleaned.

Now, as Thomas entered the hall, his boots heavy against the wooden floor, Evelyn felt the hair rise on the back of her neck. He paused near the kitchen door, rubbing the back of his neck and muttering something about the fields, and Evelyn's stomach clenched.

"You're home early," she said, her voice tighter than she intended.

Thomas glanced at her, raising an eyebrow. "Figured I'd have a quick rest before I take care of the fencing. Need to do it before the rain comes in. You all right?"

"Fine." She tried to sound breezy, but the way his eyes lingered on her face made her pulse quicken. She busied herself with the bread, slicing it into perfect, even pieces. Her hands were steady, though her heart raced.

Thomas leaned against the door frame, crossing his arms. "You've been jumpy lately," he said, his tone casual but probing.

She forced a laugh, glancing at him briefly. "Don't be silly. There's just a lot to do with the spring coming."

He grunted, his gaze flickering back to the hall and the work that waited for him beyond the back door. Evelyn resisted the urge to step between him and the trinket box on the table, knowing it would draw his suspicion. Instead, she piled a plate with bread slices and walked toward him, holding it in front of her.

"Eat something," she said. "You'll need your strength for the fencing."

Thomas hesitated, his eyes narrowing just slightly, but he grabbed a piece of bread and bit into it. "Don't know why I feel like I'm missing something around here," he muttered.

Evelyn's hand froze on the knife. She forced herself to keep slicing, her breaths shallow.

He took the plate and headed to the living room to look over the paper while he ate, and Evelyn grabbed the trinket box, stowing it safely in her apron pocket once again.

Outside, the wind picked up, rustling the bare branches of the oak tree near the window. The sound seemed louder than usual, almost mocking. Evelyn's thoughts churned as she tried to imagine what Thomas might do if he ever found the box. She had hidden it well in her room last night—though well was a relative term when it came to secrets. Apparently, she needed to keep it there and only look at it when she was alone in her bedroom when Thomas was asleep down the hall.

Later that evening, when Thomas had gone to mend the fence, Evelyn reached into her pocket and traced her fingers over the tiny carvings James had etched into the lid—a single sprig of wildflowers, small and simple, just like the bouquet he had once left on her porch.

She opened it, the faint smell of fresh wood rising from the hollow interior. Inside lay only a small folded scrap of paper, yellowed at the edges, with a single word written in James' neat handwriting: Always.

Her breath caught. She hadn't opened it since he gave it to her, not wanting to risk being caught, not even by herself. Now, as she stared at the word, a bittersweet ache filled her chest. She wanted to keep it close, to hold on to the love it symbolized, but the risk felt sharper now, more dangerous.

She slipped the paper back inside, closed the lid, and returned the box to its hiding spot on her bedroom dresser. For the things you can't say aloud. That's what he had said, but there was so much she wanted to say.

The sound of Thomas' boots on the porch startled her, and she hurried back down to the kitchen quickly, pressing her hands against her apron as if to ground herself. The back door swung open, sending a gust of cold air down the hall.

"You okay?" Thomas asked again, brushing dirt off his sleeves as he entered the kitchen. His tone was softer now, less suspicious, but Evelyn could still see the flicker of doubt in his eyes.

"Of course," she said, smiling faintly. "I'll start supper."

***

The snow had finally melted, leaving the fields a patchwork of soggy earth and brittle stalks from the last harvest. Evelyn stood at the kitchen window, her hands submerged in the warm, soapy water of the dish basin, her gaze fixed on the horizon where the Thompson farm lay, just out of sight beyond the winding dirt road.

She had resolved, not three nights ago, to turn her focus inward—to her home, her husband, and her sons. A new year demanded a new start and, with it, a redirection of her heart, no matter how it felt torn in two. Seth and Samuel's childish, carefree laughter from the living room pulled her from her thoughts, and she wiped her hands on her apron, stepping out of the kitchen.

The toddler had discovered the joy of his legs just a few weeks prior, and the world seemed like a game of exploration to him now. Evelyn watched as he toddled from one chair to the next, his tiny hands reaching for anything within grasp to hold him up. His brother cheered him on, and their laughter bubbled up. It was a sound that warmed her, even as it brought an ache she couldn't quite name.

"Careful, sweetheart," she said, swooping in as Samuel reached for the edge of the tablecloth. She caught the fabric just before he pulled it to the floor. "You're going to keep me on my toes, aren't you?"

Samuel looked up at her with wide, curious eyes—hazel flecked with green. James' eyes. Her heart stumbled at the sight. The way he tilted his head, the way his small fingers curled around hers, even the lopsided grin he gave when she scooped him up—all of it was James.

She pressed her lips to his curls, breathing in the familiar scent of milk and sun-dried linen. "You're growing too fast," she murmured, bouncing him gently on her hip. He squirmed, eager to get back down, and she set him on the floor, watching as he crawled off toward the wooden blocks scattered near the fireplace.

Evelyn sank into the chair nearest the hearth, her hands folded tightly in her lap. She had tried—tried so hard—to keep her promise to herself, to focus only on the family she had chosen to keep. But every time Samuel turned toward her, every time he laughed or frowned or furrowed his little brow, she saw James.

It wasn't just the physical resemblance. It was in the way Samuel carried himself, even in those unsteady steps he was trying to take so often these days. He had a determination about him, a spark that reminded her of the way James used to lean against the fence between their properties, his eyes sharp and full of quiet mischief as he spoke about dreams beyond the fields.

"Evelyn?" Thomas' voice startled her, and she turned to see him standing in the doorway, wiping his boots on the mat. His face was flushed from the cold, his dark eyes soft but tired.

"Samuel giving you a run for your money again?" he asked, his tone light as he nodded toward the boy, who was now stacking blocks with a level of concentration that seemed far beyond his years. Seth supervised him before grabbing a toy of his own to join in the fun.

Evelyn forced a smile. "He's curious about everything these days."

Thomas chuckled, crossing the room to ruffle Samuel's hair. "Takes after you. Always poking around, always wanting to know more." He ruffled Seth's hair next, treating both boys the same in that fair way of his.

Her chest tightened, but she nodded, keeping her gaze fixed on the children. Samuel looked up and grinned, the same lopsided grin that had undone her just moments before. She reached for her mending basket, needing something to occupy her hands.

"Dinner will be ready soon," she said, her voice steady despite the storm inside her. "Why don't you get washed up?"

When he was gone, Evelyn let out a slow breath, her fingers gripping the fabric in her lap. She had made a promise to herself, and she would keep it. She would devote herself to her family, to the life she had chosen, to the home she had built with Thomas. But as Seth and Samuel's laughter filled the room again, bright and uninhibited, she couldn't help the way her heart pulled in two directions at once.

It was going to be a long year.

Chapter Twenty-One

Dear Evelyn

March 26, 1935

Dear Evelyn,

I pray this letter finds you well, though I suspect it will stir the same emotions that sit heavy on my heart as I write. There is a finality to these words that I struggle to accept, yet I know they must be said.

When last we spoke, you shared with me the story of Thomas's reaction to the rocking horse. I could see, even through your tears, how resolute you were in your choice. You have chosen your family, Evelyn, and I cannot fault you for it. In your shoes, I might have done the same.

But understanding your decision does not quiet the longing that keeps me awake most nights. It is not only you I miss, though you are ever on my mind—it is Samuel. I see him in fleeting moments, from across the fence or as he toddles behind you in the yard. I study his little frame, the way he moves, the way he tilts his head when curious, and I know him as my own. You once told me he has my eyes, and now I cannot look at his without feeling the ache of what could have been.

I understand now that I will never have the life I once dreamed of, where he would call me "Papa" and sit on my lap to hear stories of the land. But Evelyn, I cannot ignore the yearning to be something to him, no matter how small or distant. I would not ask for much—not even for him to know the truth about who I am. But perhaps there are ways for me to leave a mark on his life. Maybe when he is older, I could teach him how to mend a fence or carve a whistle from a branch. Maybe I could simply be the neighbor who watches out for him as he grows.

You must know, Evelyn, that my love for him is as real and fierce as the love I have carried for you. It breaks me to think he will never know it.

I have made arrangements to give him the only gift I can be sure will last beyond me. When my time comes, everything I have—my home, my land, and whatever I can leave behind—will be his. My will is written, and there is no changing it. I know this gift cannot replace a father's embrace or the bond we might have shared, but it is all I have to offer. Perhaps, when the time comes, he will look upon that house and those fields and feel some small sense of belonging.

I want you to know that this decision was made with peace in my heart. I will step back, Evelyn, as much as it pains me because I respect the life you have built with Thomas. But I hope you will grant me this one solace: to know that Samuel will one day have a piece of me, even if he never knows the truth.

There are no words to capture the depth of what I feel for you, for him, and for the life we might have had. But I hope you can see it between the lines of this letter, in the pauses where my pen hovered because the weight of these truths was almost too much to bear.

Yours always,

James

Chapter Twenty-Two

The Acceptance

The farmhouse sat in silence, its rooms heavy with the memories Emma had unearthed. She stood by the parlor window, her gaze trailing the outline of the willow tree that had stood sentinel over the family for generations. The box of letters sat open on the table behind her, its contents neatly stacked but radiating the weight of lives forever changed.

She could still see the looping script of the last letter, James's words burned into her mind.

"My will is written, and there is no changing it. I know this gift cannot replace a father's embrace or the bond we might have shared, but it is all I have to offer."

Emma had read that line so many times it felt etched into her memory, yet she couldn't shake the realization that it had been there all along—in the way James had always seemed like a silent fixture in her childhood, watching over her family from the periphery.

She thought back to James's funeral, a bitterly cold winter morning when she was only thirteen. The memory felt different now, charged with a meaning that had been invisible to her younger self. She re-membered standing beside her father outside the small, unassuming chapel. The funeral had been sparsely attended—just a few neighbors, the pastor, and her family.

Her father had been strangely quiet that day, his usual stoic demeanor slipping into something almost fragile. She remembered the way his hands trembled as he folded the simple black scarf around his neck, the way he had avoided James's casket like it was something he couldn't bear to look at. At the time, Emma had chalked it up to the solemnity of death, but now, she wasn't so sure.

She turned from the window, her reflection fading as she moved back toward the letters. Sitting down, Emma let her fingers brush the delicate edges of the paper.

There had always been something about James that made him feel a little more familiar than he should have, though she hadn't been able to place it as a child. He had always been kind—quieter than her other neighbors, sure, but steady in a way that drew her attention without her realizing it.

She recalled one summer when she was seven or eight, her grandmother Evelyn had sent her to deliver a jar of blackberry preserves to Mr. Thompson's house. The dirt path that led to his front porch had been overgrown and wild, the kind of place her mother had warned her about snakes. James had answered the door with a smile, his weathered face crinkling at the corners as he crouched to her level.

"Tell your grandma thank you for me, Emma," he'd said, taking the jar with both hands as though it were something precious. "Blackberries are the best kind."

He had offered her a handful of candy from a tin on his shelf, and she had skipped home, clutching the sticky butterscotch with the kind of glee only a child could manage.

Now, thinking back to that moment, she wondered if it had meant something more to him. Did he see Evelyn in her then? Did he see himself and Samuel in her?

The weight of the realization pressed into her chest, bittersweet and inescapable. James had been there, just across the road, leaving pieces of himself in ways no one dared to name.

The letters painted a picture of a man who had loved deeply, too deeply, for the time and place they lived. A man who had accepted the boundaries Evelyn set but had never stopped trying to protect what little he could claim as his legacy. He hadn't just left his land and home to her father out of kindness; it was his way of giving Samuel, and by extension, the rest of them, what he couldn't in life.

Emma leaned back in her chair, letting her head rest against the cool wood. Her heart ached with the enormity of it all—the sacrifice, the love, and the silence that had blanketed it for so long. She wondered how her father had found out. Had Evelyn ever told him outright, or had he pieced it together from the things left unsaid?

She could still see her grandmother, years later, tending to the hydrangeas by the porch as if they were her life's work. Evelyn had always spoken fondly of James but never too much. Never more than a passing comment about how good of a neighbor he had been or how kind he was to the children.

But now, in the quiet of the old farmhouse, Emma could see it all so clearly—the secret looks, the unspoken agreements, the way the land itself seemed to hold the truth like a whispered confession.

It wasn't just James's story or Evelyn's. It was hers, too.

Emma ran her hand over the letters once more, and her decision was made. She would tell this story. Not just for James, or Evelyn, or even Samuel. She would tell it for herself, and for every piece of her family she could finally see whole.

***

The late afternoon sun poured golden light into the kitchen, catching the dust motes as they danced lazily in the air. Emma sat at the kitchen table, her grandmother's letters spread before her in a careful, reverent arc. The old farmhouse felt alive in a way it hadn't since she'd arrived, the worn floorboards and faded wallpaper heavy with the stories she had uncovered.

Her father's face hovered in her mind, clearer than it had been in years. The quiet strength of his features, the way he would stand at the edge of a room, observing, as if he didn't quite know how to fully belong. He had always been an enigma to her—steadfast, dependable, but cloaked in a reserve she had never understood.

Until now.

She traced the edge of one letter with her finger, its delicate folds soft from decades of handling. The words felt almost alive beneath her touch. James's love for Evelyn had been undeniable, even when filtered through the careful restraint of the letters. His love for Samuel, her father, was no less evident.

Emma thought back to her childhood, to the moments that had seemed so unremarkable at the time. Her father had been a man of few words, his love expressed in actions more than speech. She remembered the way he had mended her bike tirelessly one summer, his hands grease-stained and patient. The way he'd always been the first to rise and the last to sleep, ensuring the farm ran like clockwork. He had been steady, but distant—never harsh, never unkind, but always carrying something invisible that seemed to weigh him down.

Now she knew what it was.

Her father had grown up knowing the truth. Not the sanitized version her brothers had offered her when she'd confronted them, but the full truth. He had known James wasn't just the kind neighbor who helped when the tractor broke or brought over fresh peaches in the summer. He had known James was his father, but he had also known why he couldn't claim that role.

Emma stood, moving to the window. The fields stretched out before her, a patchwork of browning grasses and freshly tilled soil. Her father had walked these fields every day of his young life, she realized, knowing he carried two fathers with him: the one who raised him, and the one who could only watch from across Willow Branch Road.

How had he balanced it? How had he looked at James without bitterness or longing? Or maybe he had felt those things but had buried them so deep they had turned into the quiet stoicism she had always mistaken for apathy.

Her heart ached with the realization of it. He had been protecting Evelyn, just as James had, just as Thomas had. They had all conspired to keep this secret, not out of malice or deceit, but out of love. Love that had demanded they sacrifice their own desires, their own truths, for the sake of appearances, for the sake of stability.

And what had it cost her father?

She remembered the last time she had spoken to him, a year before his passing. They had argued—about what, she couldn't even recall now—but she had stormed off, angry at his calm, detached demeanor. He had stood on the porch, watching her leave, his hands tucked into his pockets. She hadn't noticed the sadness in his eyes then, but now she couldn't unsee it.

Emma's throat tightened as the pieces fell into place. He had carried so much, never letting it slip. Not even to her.

Her father had understood in some way, she knew. Perhaps not fully, not until he was older, but he had carried that knowledge, and it had shaped the man he became. It explained his quiet strength, his loyalty to the farm, his unspoken bond with James. It explained why he had worked so tirelessly to preserve the life Evelyn and Thomas had built, even if it wasn't the whole truth.

Emma's father had been more than she'd ever given him credit for. He had been a bridge between two lives, two loves, two worlds that had never fully collided.

And she, Emma realized, was the one willing to carry the truth forward.

***

As she packed up her belongings, finally ready to head home, back to her regular life. But would her life ever be the same again, knowing what she knew now?

As she loaded the car, the sun was setting behind the hills, casting a warm, golden glow over the farm. Emma took a minute to sit on the porch swing, the creak of its chains the only sound in the stillness. Her grandmother's letters rested on her lap, neatly tied with a fraying ribbon she'd found in the box. She didn't need to read them again—every word was etched into her memory now—but she wanted to keep them close as if they were a tether to Evelyn, to James, and to the truths they had lived but never spoken aloud.

The weight she'd carried since uncovering the DNA results had shifted, settling into something quieter, softer. At first, she'd felt betrayed, unmoored by the revelations about her family. The love she had always believed was simple and true had turned out to be tangled, complicated by choices and sacrifices she hadn't fully understood.

Now, she did.

She looked out over the fields, the horizon painted in strokes of orange and pink. This land had held all of their secrets, their joys and sorrows. Her grandmother's love for James had been real, undeniable, and powerful enough to transcend the constraints of their time. And yet, Evelyn had stayed with Thomas, had raised Samuel as his son, had chosen a life that kept the farm intact and their family whole.

Emma could see it now—the love in that choice, even in its imperfection.

The wind stirred the trees lining Willow Branch Road, their leaves rustling like whispers. She remembered walking down that road as a child, her hand in her grandmother's. Evelyn had always seemed so composed, so unshakable. But now, Emma could see the complexity beneath that calm exterior. Her grandmother hadn't been unshakable; she'd simply learned to carry her burdens with grace.

And James—Emma exhaled slowly. She thought of the man who had always seemed like a quiet presence in her life. She remembered the way he'd smiled at her from across the fence, his face weathered but kind, the way he'd handed her a basket of peaches one summer, his eyes soft with something she now recognized as longing.

He had loved them all—Evelyn, Samuel, and even her and her brothers, in the way he could. His love had been patient, enduring, content to exist in the shadows if it meant protecting them.

Emma's fingers brushed the edge of the letters, her gaze fixed on the distant tree line. She could feel the peace settling in, a steady warmth replacing the ache of confusion and anger. She didn't have to forgive them—not Evelyn, not James—because there was nothing to forgive. They had loved deeply, fiercely, and in the only way they knew how.

It wasn't the kind of love that fit neatly into stories, with tidy endings and clear rights or wrongs. But it was real, and it was enough.

Chapter Twenty-Three

The Legacy of Love

The city hummed softly outside Emma's window, a stark contrast to the quiet of the Tennessee farm she had left behind. She sat cross-legged on her worn couch, a journal spread open on her lap. The steady rhythm of rain against the glass blurred the neon glow of the streetlights below. Her pen hovered, poised yet hesitant, over the blank page while her thoughts twisted and tangled like roots deep in the earth.

Evelyn and James. Their names felt heavier now, weighted with everything she had uncovered. In the stillness of her apartment, the letters she had read seemed to whisper again. Evelyn's precise handwriting, filled with longing and heartbreak, painted vivid pictures in her mind.

Emma drew in a breath, letting it out slowly. How did one reconcile love like that? A love so powerful it bent the rules of morality and propriety, yet so quiet it stayed hidden for decades, slipping between the cracks of everyday life unnoticed.

She reached for her mug of tea, now lukewarm, and cradled it in her hands, thinking how Evelyn and James hadn't just kept a secret—they had lived a legacy. One that had shaped Emma's father, her brothers, and now her.

Emma set the mug down and ran her fingers over her journal's empty page. She didn't need the letters in front of her to feel their weight. They were etched in her memory now.

Her grandmother's choice to keep the love affair a secret wasn't just about shame or survival. It was about preserving what mattered most—her family. James's quiet acceptance of his role, forever the man so close by on Willow Branch Road, wasn't about weakness but strength. They had loved in ways Emma was only beginning to understand.

She thought about her father—his stoic silence whenever the past came up. She thought about her brothers—their quiet acceptance of truths she was just now uncovering. And then she thought about the next generation—the stories her nieces and nephews would inherit, the way their family history would be framed.

Could she keep it to herself? Tuck the letters back into the box and leave them there, as Evelyn had done for so long? Or should she share it—honor their love and sacrifices by giving their story a voice?

A memory flickered in her mind of sitting on the porch of the farmhouse as a child, Evelyn's steady hands braiding her hair. "We all make choices," her grandmother had said, though Emma couldn't remember the context. "But it's what we do with them after that makes us who we are."

Emma smiled faintly at the thought. Evelyn's choices had made her brave. Maybe hers could do the same.

She reached for her laptop, pulling it onto her knees. With one last glance at the journal, she opened a blank document. The cursor blinked, waiting. Emma hesitated for only a moment before she began typing.

"This is a love story. But it isn't simple…"

The words spilled out, filling the page, as Emma felt the weight of her grandmother's legacy settle into something else entirely—a purpose.

***

The light from Emma's desk lamp cast a warm glow, creating soft pools of gold against the darkened corners. She had spent many of her waking hours writing the love story her grandmother had lived. It had poured out of her so easily that she almost felt like it was her own story. It made her understand her grandmother in a whole new way, and she hoped what she'd written had done her justice.

But now it was time to face the music. She wanted to re-read the document she'd written and see what she had put down on paper. Had she spilled her family's secrets in a way that cast them in a bad light? Would her brothers get angry at her, or would they roll their eyes and accuse her of digging up ancient history again, the way they'd seemed annoyed by her wanting to seek out the truth in the first place?

She had her notebook open next to her, ready to write down anything that stood out to her from what she'd written. Lines she thought might cause her brothers to raise their eyebrows. Or things that might point too clearly to their family. She wanted to muddy the details just enough so it wouldn't be obvious but still allow her grandmother's love to shine through.

Emma's gaze drifted to the window, where the glass reflected a faint silhouette of her face. She studied her own eyes, the line of her mouth, the arch of her brows. She had always assumed these traits came from her grandparents' shared lineage, a seamless blend of Evelyn and Thomas Harris. But now, every glance in the mirror made her wonder. How much of James was there in her? In her restless drive, her longing for something she couldn't quite name?

She closed her eyes and let her mind wander back to the farm, to the quiet mornings spent in her grandmother's kitchen, the smell of coffee and fresh biscuits filling the air. She remembered Evelyn's hands—soft but steady—folding dough, shelling peas, braiding her hair. Those hands had written letters filled with heartbreak and longing, and yet they had also built a life that was strong and enduring. A life that had sheltered Emma, her brothers, and their father, even as it hid its deepest truths.

Her pen hovered over the notebook again, this time trembling slightly. What had Evelyn been thinking the first time she put her feelings for James into words? The question felt too big to answer, but she let herself imagine it—the loneliness of loving someone you couldn't have, the fear of losing everything if the secret ever came out.

And yet, Evelyn had chosen love. Chosen it quietly, fiercely, even when it could never be fully hers.

Love wasn't clean or easy. It wasn't always fair. But it was enduring. Evelyn and James had proven that, even in the silence they had left behind.

Emma scrolled through the first pages of her manuscript, her fingers lingering on the keyboard without pressing any keys. The words stared back at her, rich with emotion and yet carefully veiled, truth carefully woven into a fabric of fiction. She read the opening paragraph aloud, her voice breaking the stillness of the room. The sentences flowed like music, but she couldn't help listening for discordant notes, anything that might sound too personal, too raw, too revealing.

Her grandmother's name had been changed, and the name of the road separating their farms was different now, though it still evoked the same wistful imagery: a forgotten stretch of land where love had taken root. But it wasn't the names or places she worried about; it was the heart of the story. The moments when the veil between fiction and truth felt too thin, as if Evelyn's voice might suddenly whisper through the pages.

Pausing, Emma ran her hand over the notebook beside her, its pages half-filled with scribbled notes and second-guessing. She had highlighted a scene near the middle—her grandmother sitting at her writing desk, her hand trembling over the paper as she penned a letter she knew she shouldn't send. "I never meant to love you," the letter began. Emma's throat tightened as she re-read the line. She had written it, but it didn't feel like hers. It felt plucked from Evelyn's heart, from a place she hadn't meant to share but couldn't keep hidden.

Her pen moved across the notebook's margin: Too much? Too close? She stared at the question, biting the inside of her cheek. The balance was delicate—giving the story its emotional weight without tipping into betrayal.

For a moment, Emma considered deleting the scene entirely, but she couldn't bring herself to do it. The letter was fictional, but the sentiment wasn't. Evelyn's life had been filled with words she couldn't say, feelings she couldn't name. It felt wrong to erase even the imagined echoes of them.

Instead, she leaned back in her chair, her eyes scanning the ceiling. She needed to decide. Not just what to keep or cut but whether she could let this story go at all. Would the world see the love she had tried to honor? Or would they only see the scandal buried beneath it?

The only way out was through, she knew, and so she turned back to the document and kept reading as the night outside her window grew darker.

As the sun rose the next morning, Emma closed her laptop with a quiet click, her heart steady now in a way it hadn't been before. She had read every word and every sentence and felt their weight settle into place like pieces of a puzzle that was finally complete. The story wasn't perfect—she knew that—but it was honest in the ways that mattered. It captured the love her grandmother had held in secret, the sacrifices made in silence, and the enduring strength of bonds forged against impossible odds. With her final notes scribbled in the margins of her notebook and the last line of the manuscript etched in her mind, Emma felt ready. It was time for the world to see what she had seen, to feel what she had felt. Time for others to understand that even love hidden in the shadows could burn bright enough to shape generations.

Epilogue: Telling the Story

E mma hit send and leaned back in her chair, exhaling a long breath she hadn't realized she was holding. The email, addressed to her literary agent, carried the final draft of her novel—a story born of whispers, secrets, and the fragile threads of truth interwoven through a fictitious love story. The subject line read simply: *Final Draft: Willow Branch Road.*

The cursor blinked at her from the now-empty email screen as if waiting for her to second-guess herself, to reach out and grab the story back. But she didn't. It was done. The weight of it—the words, the emotions, the carefully constructed veil of fiction—settled over her like a well-worn quilt, heavy but comforting.

Her desk was cluttered with evidence of the journey that had brought her to this point. A stack of old photographs, faded and curling at the edges, sat beside the letters she had found on her grandmother's farm. Those letters had been the foundation of her story, the lifeline to Evelyn and James's quiet, forbidden love.

But her book wasn't their story, not exactly. She had changed so much about it: the names, settings, places, timelines. She had built new characters out of the raw material of their lives, honoring the truth without exposing any of it. It was, in every way that mattered, a love letter to the past—to her grandparents and the impossible choices they had made to protect their family.

Her phone buzzed on the desk, and Emma glanced down at the notification. It was a simple reply from her agent: *Got it. What a story, Emma! This one's going to resonate.*

Resonate. The word settled in her chest like a small ember, warm and steady. She hoped it would. Hoped that the fictionalized tale of love, sacrifice, and resilience would touch readers without betraying the legacy of the people who had lived it.

Emma stood at the edge of Willow Branch Road, the farmhouse a silhouette against the golden light of the setting sun. The fields stretched endlessly before her, their quiet beauty a testament to generations of hard work and sacrifice. She traced her fingers over the letters she had found, now carefully tucked back into their hiding place, their secrets safe once more.

She smiled softly, her heart swelling with a mix of pride and gratitude. The stories she uncovered weren't just tales of love and loss—they were proof of the strength her family had carried through the years, even when faced with choices that weren't easy. She felt a profound respect for the sacrifices her grandmother had made and for the wisdom to understand that some truths were better left unsaid.

The name she carried, *Emma Harris,* wasn't her true surname, but it didn't feel any less hers. It was a blanket that had shielded her family's secret, a legacy woven from both courage and fragility. She realized now that the name wasn't about blood or lineage—it was about the love and determination that held her family together, even in silence.

Looking out over the farm, Emma felt a deep sense of belonging. She wasn't just a part of the family's story—she was part of its legacy. The truth she had uncovered didn't break that legacy; it only made it richer. Her grandmother's love, though hidden, was unbreakable. Its fragile beauty lay in the way it endured, unseen yet ever present, shaping the lives of those who came after.

The love story was out of her hands now, but the people it honored were not forgotten. In writing their love, she had found her own peace—a sense of connection to a history that had once felt distant and unknowable. As a breeze rustled the trees along the road, Emma whispered, "I'm proud to be part of this." She felt the weight of the past settle comfortably on her shoulders, not as a burden but as a gift. The secret was safe, the legacy was intact, and for Emma, that was enough.

She turned toward the farmhouse, her steps light with purpose. This place, with all its history and heartache, was her home—not because of the name it bore but because of the love it carried. And that love, as fragile as it might have seemed, was stronger than anything she could have imagined.

www.ingramcontent.com/pod-product-compliance
Lightning Source LLC
Chambersburg PA
CBHW020636110726
47899CB00002B/792